To my soulmate Karen without whom I would not be here.

A

Although there were many emotions I could have used for the letter A such as ambitious, altruistic, and one of my personal favorites, aberrant. I chose to go with anger as I can find no living person on this planet that is NOT subject to its effects.

You cannot tell me that even in the misty Buddhist temples of Nepal there isn't a single monk that has at one time, awaken, swung his legs out of bed, stepped into a pile of goat shit, slipped and stubbed his toe on the stone wall, and he does not get angry? Not bloody likely.

And, like any well-meaning, unknowing civilization such as our own, we have screwed up the concept of anger to the complete confusion of all. There is the anger of disappointment, the anger of retribution, and another of my personal favorites, just plain old *pissed off.* More seriously, anger is a dangerous flaw and leads to the absence of reason when reason is usually exactly what is needed. Anger is also mandatory in some instances. Name one? How about when someone says or does something hurtful to a smaller or weaker individual? Then you BETTER get angry!

Affability is the second emotion represented. Being affable is not as easy as it looks. Wanting to be liked is a feeling which I believe everyone has in varying degrees. I figured out long ago that it's not important that people like you, only that they respect who you are and what you stand for. Likeability also hinges many times on the superfluous: hair, eyes, body shape, etc. What has always sealed the deal for me is when a beautiful woman laughs. And I don't mean that oh-tee-hee-hand-cupped over mouth dainty debutante chuckle. I'm talking about that deep-from-the-belly-truck driver roar that makes you do the double-take. Give me a woman who is not afraid to laugh out loud any day.

Sexy.

******

My Furry Friend

He was, without a doubt, the absolute best friend I ever had. Only 2.7 pounds on the day I bought him, his first taste of cool, yummy milk was taken from a 1oz. sauce ramekin. He was *tiny*. On the way home from the breeder's house and the warmth and security of his dwindling family, I kept saying the name that came to me as I saw him scooting through the back yard with his brother and sister, the last two remaining pups from the litter.

Scooter.

Five-week-old Scooter used all the warmth and energy in his body to make the climb up my chest to a nice warm neck just above. Once there, he curled up in a tight little ball and settled in for the ride to his new home.

"Hello there small and furry friend," I cooed. "Hello Scooter!"

He responded by letting out a small puff of air from his black Jujube of a nose.

The love affair was on.

Scooter went everywhere with me. We would hit the beach in the morning; avoiding crowds and allowing Scooter free reign on this whole stretch of Pacific surf for as far as he could see. Puppy paradise. Once East Beach started filling up with the usual assortment of tourists, bums, and millionaires, we would make our way home.

Feed Scooter. Check. Beer. Check. Joint. Check….

Ready for our next adventure…..

Scooter was starting to get a little pouch of a belly from being spoiled rotten, so he propped his rotund little body up on the couch arm, staring longingly at his hopeful destination. I leaned down, cupped his little butt in my hand and gently placed him on his favorite Moo Cow Blankee. It was soft, warm, and Cassie had bought it for him on his first birthday.

Cassie. That made two girls that had left me in the last four months. Wonder what *their* problems were?

Scooter didn't care about Cassie. Or Lisa. Or Sarah. Or Shannon. He knew without a doubt, his dad would take care of him. On *that* he could always depend. As we made our way up the 101 north to Goleta, I saw a small stretch of smooth beach and not a parked car in sight. Since this alone was a rarity, I pulled over. Scooter, his head just clearing the bottom of the window, yelped as his stubby tail started wiggling uncontrollably. As I eased my '65 Impala to a stop, the whining and excitement mounted as Scooter pawed at the armrest to get out.

"Go get 'em boy!" I shouted. From the floorboard he leapt and landed with a small *oomph*. Off to the surf he bounded with the exuberance and innocence all puppies possess. We spent the next three hours by ourselves, playing in the water. After some swimming, fetch, and just plain rolling around in the sand, I glanced at my watch.

"Oh shit. We're running late," I said out loud. "Let's go Scooter. Band practice."

Six more months passed by and the reason I knew that calculation is because two more women had come and gone. But there was my little buddy Scooter with his soulful brown eyes that danced and almost made him look like he was laughing. He jumped on the couch beside me and then sort of eased his way onto my lap. As I began scratching the back of his neck, his rear right leg started kicking involuntarily.

"Kick start! Kick start!" Scooter rolled over on his back and let out a puppy-sigh that signaled the onset of sleep. I lay my head back on the cool black leather upholstery. Off we drifted….

God has truly blessed us with animals such as cats and dogs. The problem is they just don't live long enough. I don't imagine I will ever be without a dog. I absolutely love them. They are the most loyal and appreciative of beings and cute beyond words. I bristled and twitched, awakened by a little pink tongue eagerly wetting my right cheek. Someone was hungry as indicated by the Stubby Tail Food Dance.

Scooter barked at the intruder as I opened the pantry door. I instinctively ducked as I saw a shadow looming, but my head exploded, and darkness descended. I was out cold for over an hour. As the din subsided, an insufferable pounding forced my eyes shut. I stumbled to my feet and ran to the open back door. I did not see my constant companion anywhere. The house was feeling cold as the outside air blew in.

"Scooter!" I screamed at the top of my lungs. I could feel dried blood crack on my skin as I shouted. My little buddy was nowhere in sight. Blindly, I rushed through the dark to find him. At that single, solitary moment, all I could think about was my doggy's safety. I crossed the street into a neighborhood foreign to me, and as my eyes adjusted to the night, my heart jumped.

"Scooter!" I shouted in glee as I approached my little boy.

`As I gazed skyward, one thought screamed in my head and has every day from that day forward: I will *never* rest until I find the cold-hearted bastard that slit the throat of my furry little friend, leaving him to die here cold, alone, and afraid, in a strange, dark place.

******

Little Things

I wanted to interview Thomas Coley ever since I first heard of his amazing story. My editor was a little less enthusiastic but had agreed to let me do it for a piece in the "People in the News" segment which ran weekly in our newspaper. So I grabbed my recorder, a small pocket-sized model with the little three-inch cassettes my mother had given me on the day I got my job here. For her, this was the culmination and payoff for the meager seven years of college I spent to get my journalism degree, and she was bursting with questions when I told her of my impending meeting the next day with Thomas.

"What is the first question you are going to ask?" she bubbled.

I thought for a second and kept reminding myself *don't forget the little things. The big picture stuff will take care of itself.*

"Well. I thought I'd start with…."

She didn't wait for the reply, obviously star-struck at her daughter meeting, interviewing, and writing a story on a real honest-to-goodness celebrity.

"He is drop-dead gorgeous! She exclaimed. That is one fine-looking man," she added.

"Mom, you have to remember"… I tried to inject, but she was having none of it. She was already on the phone with her best friend and bridge partner Marge detailing my assignment including (for the third time) the phrase "drop-dead gorgeous." I took one last swig of my Venti Latte with an extra shot of expresso and headed out for Marion. Just west of Marion was Carbondale, home of the Crab Orchard National Wildlife Refuge, and beautiful Crab Orchard Lake. I made a mental note to stop by there for a picnic lunch when I finished my interview.

Five hours later, I arrived in Marion, stopping at a mom-and-Pop burger joint to grab a snack which included a delicious vanilla shake to help quell the nervous stomach I had developed. I guess I was star-struck or nervous after all, I admitted to myself. I finished in a hurry and closed the door with the rusty little bell jingling behind me as I exited.

So there we sat, the cub reporter and the movie star looking across the table at each other in silence. As much as it hurt to admit it, my mother was right. He *was* drop-dead gorgeous. But as I began, what really struck me was how genuinely nice he was. Down-to-earth and approachable, with a square jaw and perfect white teeth. His blue eyes penetrated the very core of my soul.

"Tell me something most people would never know about you, I began. What was your childhood like? Were you happy growing up?" People loved this human-interest stuff. Journalism 101.

Get the subject talking about themselves and then hit them with the big questions. *Don't forget the little things.*

He showed no signs of being uncomfortable with my first salvo of questions and slowly began speaking. Perfect diction, perfect delivery, and of course, perfect white teeth.

"My parents provided me with every opportunity to succeed, he began. My childhood was a very happy, loving time, so no headline-grabbing revelations available there," he offered almost apologetically. "My two elder siblings were somewhat over-protective of me, so I led quite the sheltered existence," he recounted wistfully. "I always had a pet when I was growing up, a fish, a bird, I didn't quite care what, but I was always surrounded by animals, so I grew up protecting them. That is why…"

"You give so much of your time and money to different animal charities and organizations," I finished his sentence.

"You've done your homework," he complimented. He expounded "that is also why I ONLY give my time and money to animal organizations."

My raised eyebrow must have belied my relaxed posture, so Thomas felt the need to continue. "Let me ask you something," he began. "Have you ever had a dog tell you a lie? Have you ever had a cat try to steal your money at gunpoint? Has a bird ever broken into your house and stolen your stereo or television?"
"Neither have I," he said before I could proffer an answer to any of his questions. His eyes were narrowing into a laser-like stare as I really started to feel self-conscious

"Neither have I."

He went on about his happy childhood, his climb to film stardom, and I found myself both in awe and in love. I felt my cheeks flush. I gathered myself and started. I also realized my allotted time had come to an end. I blurted as he began to rise.

"Thomas, you are one of the most visible faces on the planet. Admired by men. Adored by women. Idolized by millions. Where do you go to escape it all?"

"Really?" he laughed. "Let me guess. First ever interview for you, right?"

Now I was blushing crimson. I nodded.

"Well, you might have taken into consideration the fact that you are conducting this interview in a federal maximum-security prison and that I am shackled by the legs and handcuffed to this chair. Or the fact that I disemboweled six people and ate their intestines."

"You know, little things like that."

******

B

I was thinking about writing a story under the blameless emotion, but also flirted with brutal, bullied, and ballistic. I settled on bashful as the illustration. I remember being bashful on numerous occasions growing up. I recall the recurring dream I had when I was five. I would wake up, get dressed, eat breakfast, and go to school. I remember looking at my classmates and they were smiling and laughing. I looked down and *I was completely naked!*

Insecurity.

My family traveled so I was constantly changing schools and charged with always having to make new friends. However, I also found that the same thing making me bashful allowed me later to become the talk-first, think-second idiot I am today.

This is probably the core reason I have always gone for the weird and shocking. Others may find it colorful and interesting. Right.

I hate the feeling of betrayal. It lends itself to bad thoughts of retaliation on some imaginary scoreboard somewhere.

Weak.

Another of my "areas of opportunity" would have to be in the fact that I am way too trusting of people. I find that as I age, the less trusting I have become. That sucks. I was the original hippie love and peace guy. Now, I view every person who approaches my front door as a potential serial killer arriving at
their next job site. I have very laissez-faire thoughts about people who take another's life. I believe every citizen of the world starts out holding the same basic human rights. The right to be noticed, heard, and respected. The right to legal protection. Fair trial, all of it. BUT I also firmly believe once you take another's life, you forfeit any and all societal rights and protections. I am a Code of Hammurabi guy and always marveled at how much paperwork (and trees) would have been saved if our legal system adhered to the simple "eye-for-an-eye" concepts of the Code. Steal something-lose a hand, stab someone-get stabbed in return, and we will not even talk about rape.

Conversely, I have always put a premium on loyalty as I have navigated my life path, and I can look no further for evidence of it than my soulmate wife Karen. The things that woman has endured…Loyalty I will be forever grateful for. You cannot disguise it, only appreciate it. I'm sure when she reads this, she will come up with another word starting with b (and ending in u-l-l-s-h-i-t).

******

Speak up!

Rose Cavanaugh was absolutely beautiful beyond words and Dom Filleri worshipped the ground she walked on. Her eyes made him laugh inwardly and although physical contact did not seem like an option, he could not wait to see her every day. As she sat in the garden she read and enjoyed the dapples of sunlight snaking their way through the leaves of the Ficus trees. Her graceful white flesh peeked out at the waning sunlight as she read. Dom swore to himself that if he ever got the chance, even the slightest *possibility* of a chance, he was going to throw convention aside, walk right up to her, and hold her closely to his beating heart. He would cover her lips with his own and embrace her the way only two lovers-to-be can. He was consumed by her: her voice, her

smell, her warm countenance. Not a day passed without
the same longing and yearning returning to remind him of his frail human condition. He was slowly, inevitably, reaching a point of no return. He had to say something or do something, anything, to let her know how he felt. His days were filled with stolen glances and undeciphered signals, and his nights were spent bringing himself to the very precipice of physical exhaustion. *Enough*, he said to himself. *Tomorrow it is*. He was worried he would place their work relationship at risk, but one unavoidable, undeniable fact kept coursing through his body: he <u>had</u> to have her! As he approached, she glanced up from reading and their eyes met.

"Sister Rose? He asked. "Can I see you in the Rectory?"

"Yes, Father Dominic. I will be right there."

******

C

A lot of awesome emotions under "C" and I moved the location to Canada, one of my favorite places to visit. On one salmon fishing trip there, my father, sister, and I were enjoying a great day of drinking. Not so much on the fishing part of the fishing trip. After a case or so of Labatt's Blue and a liter of Dr. McGillicuddy's 100-proof Peach Schnapps, we were ready to start drinking some more. At least that was the plan. This is where the story becomes a little fuzzy.

I woke up at about 2am (I think) and the first thing I noticed was my eyes were wide open and I could not see anything. Only darkness. Was I blind? I turned my baseball cap around and my sight was miraculously restored. The next thing that assaulted my senses was the horrendous smell of shit. As I propped my throbbing head up on one elbow, I reached back to rub my aching spine which was partially resting on a bed of pinecones. As I rubbed, my fingers found the slimy stench beginning on the top of my pants.

Oh my God, I crapped myself!

This was not good.

Pan to me pounding on my sister's cabin. Her lover got up and helped me to the washroom cabin.

"I'm a senior citizen, I shat myself," I shouted as she sprayed me off with a hose. After cleaning me off, she threw me a towel, and I kept yelling my thanks as she returned to her cabin.

I toweled off, and as I peeled off my soaked but clean clothes, I saw that there was no evidence whatsoever of any excrement *inside* my pants.

I have never been so proud to have gotten blind-drunk and fallen asleep in a big pile of bearshit in my entire life.

******

Criminal

The hulking figure stealthily crossed the cinnamon-red Spanish tile, approached the door, and froze.

"Hands in the air! Do it *NOW*!" The unmistakable click of the Glock 22 .40 Cal pierced the black silence as one of the fifteen live rounds readied for firing. The handgun was issued to Inspector Ron Lewis of the local police. It had never been fired in its five-year career on the force.

"Be cool, be cool. See I'm putting my hands…."

A swift strike of the nightstick cracked one of the large man's ribs and forced him to his hands and knees. The man gasped, fought unconsciousness, lost, and fell to the carpeted floor in a *thud*.

The house looked like a drug dealer lived there. Talk about excess. In the foyer, a marbled koi pond meandered through the Great Room to the pool outside. Its serpentine route wound lazily past two twin white baby grand Akai pianos on its way to a majestic two-story waterfall. This provided a refreshing twenty-five-foot drop for the fat carp and their fellow *nishikigoi*. The pond then circled the indoor gym, sauna, and steam room, before rejoining the main pond in the home theater. On top of a marble bar was $476,878 neatly stacked. On one of the covered pool tables sat several scales of various sizes. Everything was

coated with a fine white powder, making Ron
think of what a nuclear residue must look like. On
another pool table, large empty Pyrex lab flasks sat
waiting for their turn as the apparatus in the center
of the room belched smoke and sweet ether.
Alternating with the distinctive odor of cat-urine
which all meth labs produce, Ron just shook his
head as the three overhead fans drew the smoke up
to within the top ten feet of the ceiling, lurking
there in an ominous, poisonous cloud.

Ron looked around, absorbing it all. This
was the kind of money he had always dreamed of
when he was growing up. Beautiful house, pool,
three foreign cars parked in the garage.

Oh well, he mused……He heard a knock at
the door.

Special Constable Bill Shulte arrived on the
scene and jostled the dark man on the front porch
to his feet. He roughly cuffed him, enjoying every
minute of it.

Bill and Ron were childhood friends who
were now growing up together in
their respective police careers.

"Thanks for coming by Billy. I owe you
one."

"You owe me a lot more than one, mate. Bill
shoved the suspect's face into the door. Who the
hell is this guy?"

"Beats me mate. Caught him breaking into
my house."

******

D

Almost all the cool emotions are under the letter D such as depression (way too easy) and defeatist, but I went with despair. We will all, but a select few of us, suffer despair in our short time in this sphere of existence and it can be silently or screamingly endured. Of those two, I prefer the former. Just about anything can be placed under the dangerous emotion including my two Cocker Spaniel pups tearing through the house at warp speed.

I also liked the emotion daffy. Now answer truthfully have you ever heard the word daffy used outside of Daffy Duck, my constant childhood TV companion?

Me neither.

The Brits use daft which basically means the same thing. I believe I was descended from a British landholder in Mexico, but no supporting documentation, only family remembrances.

I love the British, especially the sports commentators. I'm a Manchester United fan, the first game I watched being Man U v West Bromwich Albion in 1967. Georgie Best, Bobby Charlton, Nobby Stiles. Great team.

We play soccer in our country and everyone else plays football. Maybe that's why we are always getting our asses kicked in international competitions?

Easy ladies, I was just getting to your "badass selves" as our ex-Commander-in-Chief might have said. Seriously mad props to the U.S. Women's National Team!

In England, when a soccer (football) player misses a shot on goal it's not the end of the world, only "hard cheese."

Doesn't get much harsher than that.

When I lived in Jolly Old there was one American TV show---*Rowan and Martin's Laugh-In.* The one glimpse the British had into who we yanks are, and what we stand for. With apologies to yummy little Goldie Hawn in her bikini and slogan-painted body, no wonder they think we are so messed up!

You Millennial Googlers: "sock it to me!"

The story I chose depicts life as one person lived it, south of the border.

******

Mexican Vacation

Dave lay perfectly still on the cool adobe floor. He kept his eyes shut and listened to the infected rats shuffling across his cell. He could hear the screams of the former occupants of this six-by-six hell hole. In Spanish or English, it didn't matter; horror was horror in any language. He forced open the swollen slits he called eyes. Damn, he thought as they fought for light. His disappointment grew as they opened and remained open. Oh well, another beautiful day in La Paz, Baja California.

Outside the chalky, bleached-white walls, *turistas* laughed, guzzled down watered-down margaritas, and posed for silly pictures wearing oversized sombreros. They gobbled down boiled *camarrones* as big as your fist and swayed rhythmically to the mariachi renditions of traditional Mexican folk songs.

Inside the rotting yellow interior walls Dave's heart continued to vomit thick blood, keeping him alive one more day. In the corner sat what remained of yesterday's rice and beans, processed through his bleeding bowels. Next to the fly-riddled mass, the leaking bowl of liquid mocked him.

Come on, Dave. Drink it. I know the guards pissed and spit into it again, but you've got to stay alive. Only eight more months.

Dave raised the greasy tin bowl to his lips and drained it.

Eight more months. His original sentence of six years had grown to ten years and eight months for defending his virgin anus from a drunken prison guard. He wondered why he bothered at all. He remained a "virgin" for only two more weeks and then….Dave knelt over his own shit and puked what remained of his roiling guts all over the surprised flies. Yeah, he thought. Another beautiful day in La Paz, Baja California.

All this for a couple kilos of cheap Mexican weed. Such a deal for Pretty Boy Dave. If no WHEN he got out, he was heading back to Laguna Beach and some ten-foot glassy California surf. He couldn't wait; but he had to. Only eight more months, he thought to himself.

Dave limped into the barren courtyard while the guards sprayed his walls down, but the stench never got washed away. It was Dave's only friend and constant companion.

In the following seven months and twenty-nine days, Pretty Boy Dave Willows was raped twelve times, four times by inmates and eight by the guards. His two front teeth were knocked from his head in yet another vain attempt to protect what little remained
his dignity. He drank at least two hundred more bowls of piss and spit water, got diarrhea twenty-five times, and dreamed of his beloved Laguna Beach every second of his miserable existence.

Dave didn't sleep at all on his last night in the cell; the guards saw to that. Afterwards, Dave limped back to his cell, but he was still focused on his departure. He regaled his rat friends with one last story: The Triumphant Return of Pretty Boy Dave Willows.

Daybreak found Dave smiling and enjoying the unique ambience that had been his palace for the last ten years and eight months. Lindo, the most abusive of his jailers, leered lustily at Dave and cackled.

"*Odalay precioso*, how you like it last night? You gonna miss Big Lindo?" His maniacal laugh echoed throughout the soon-to-be-empty cell.

Yeah, I'm gonna miss you, you bean-sucking asshole. I'm gonna miss you a lot. Dave grinned and stumbled on.

Dave was numb as he was marched across the dusty courtyard for the last time. To home. Freedom. He would be issued a one-way bus ticket to El Paso, Texas. USA. Freedom. He was so numb, in fact, that he didn't even feel the slimy hands of Lindo as he pulled Dave to him and whispered in his ear.

"You come back and see me *pollo*. Lindo love you mucho."

Dave was oblivious to everyone and everything including the chunk of black tar heroin that Lindo had slipped into his pocket.

Dave turned to Lindo and the other guards and smiled. *Oh well, kiss my white ass, I am outta here*, he thought. "Hasta la whatever" was what came out.

Pretty Boy Dave Willows, with a grand total of eleven teeth, was all smiles as he headed for the main jail where he would be strip-searched one last time in front of the warden.

Another beautiful day in La Paz, Baja California.

******

E

Nothing like getting caught with your hand in the cookie jar.

Certainly not gender specific.

Economical is an emotion I never or rarely, exercised as a young man. I marvel at the person who brags about the sales price they paid for an item even though I had the same ability to get the reduced price. If I would have just bothered to look. Mainly due to laziness and the fact that the women in my life have always babied me, I always buy as opposed to shop, and usually the product that was packaged the coolest or that was the most eye-appealing.

Weak.

Stupidity is another factor in my wastefulness. Remember those old lint rollers with adhesive sheets wrapped around a plastic roller? No one ever told me there was actually sheets *under* the original one, so I would use up the first sheet until it was solid with lint, flotsam, jetsam, etc., and then I would simply throw it away. I remember thinking *man; those things are expensive and don't last very long.*

Kind of like girlfriends.

If you want to see a *real* Master of Economy, look no further than the nearest working mother of three. Talk about making magic.

My brother and I worked in the culinary field. We actually tried collaborating on a few occasions, but it was doomed from the very start. See, Ed thought he was the world's greatest chef and I *knew* I was. I owe much of my inventiveness and adaptability to my mom and her creativity in the kitchen with a limited budget. If you are not economically-minded in the food service industry, you are not in the food service industry, at least not for long. I lasted the better part of three decades, so I was doing something right, I suppose.

In today's world, being economical is even more necessary than ever. It is hard enough to make it on this planet with no money. In the interest of brevity, I will not delve into any horror stories of bankrupt sports millionaires or lottery winners and the problems they face. I have very inappropriate thoughts when I think of such waste.

******

Perfect Fit

It was a sleepy Sunday morning, and my friend-for-a-night was stirring in the next room. I guzzled down the last of my arm beer, fired up another joint, and dared a peak into the gilded mirror.

Man, I really could have done without *that*. I rubbed my swollen bloodshot eyes and stumbled back to the front room. I plopped my weary body into the blue beanbag chair and reached for the cooler. The *cooler?* What the hell was a beer cooler doing on my Persian carpet? A family legacy, the magnificent rug was an instant reminder I was supposed to "mount and secure" the carpet per Lloyd's of London Insurance. I forgot. I picked up the cooler and checked underneath. Dry. Nothing else of concern. The carpet was fine. Big sigh of relief. *I will definitely take care of this today.*

The sun tried fighting its way through the early morning marine-layer along the coast but lost the war when it reached my dusty back-door kitchen curtains. It was still pretty dark for nine in the morning. I was sipping my morning coffee in a vain attempt to get the day started. I reached for the magazine on the coffee table and started flipping through the glossy pages of models with perfect smiles.

Now this is one that looks good. It is cut to show off my six-pack and pecs I've been training so hard to get. Oh wait. No, maybe this one. My ass would look outrageous in that one…Hold on, stop the presses. If I wear THIS one I will definitely……

"Hey, Dan, are you coming back to bed?" she asked sleepily. "What are you doing going through my lingerie mag? Are you buying me something?"

She was standing in the doorway.
I looked over at her. I'd forgotten how smoking-hot she was.

Focus Daniel-san. Focus.

******

Point of View

It was a squalid, cramped two-room apartment perched over a rusty garage roof but it looked to Dylan like a *tomb*. The cleaning agents under the stained white sink emitted all the ambience of an autopsy lab. The small sliver of light peeking through the dingy curtains illuminated his last real view of this planet. If only he could untie himself and remove the sticky duct tape that was choking off what few breaths he had left. Maybe he could crawl…maybe…someone would hear him!

Maybe someone would save him from the Beast.

The door was sealed; the wooden planks across it were nailed tight as a… …coffin.

In the other room, the Beast slept soundly.

Dylan's mind was racing now, his temples pounding. He had about fifteen minutes of sunlight left. The Beast would be waking soon. As he pondered his waning existence, the cold gray walls mocked his every thought.

On the stained Formica countertop, a chopping block with sharp cutting instruments lay agonizingly out of reach. He stretched every last fiber of his body, straining to make the slightest of contact. If only….they could free him from this madness. He tried to control his breath, rushing from his lungs in a *whoosh*. Shit.

Time was running out.

The dingy flowered sofa cover would most likely serve as my death shroud, he thought. This was not the way he wanted to leave this world. Not by a long shot.

In the other room, the Beast stirred to life. She was terrifyingly calm, almost surgical in her carriage and demeanor. The powder-white walls made her smile.

This was *home.*

Her sparkling little kitchen always smelled clean and fresh. She had nailed the door shut so they could be alone. *All* alone. Away from prying eyes and distractions.

Distractions like **her.**

The new French curtains she bought saw to it they would not be disturbed. She enjoyed the thought of the great bargain she got, paying only a few dollars for them. Singing a little ditty she just could not seem to get out of her head, she calmly walked to the counter, stepping over Dylan's broken legs. She picked up her favorite boning knife and plunged it deep into her husband's chest, blood gushing out in a two-foot fountain.

"I told you if you ever cheated on me, I would kill you!" the Beast wailed.

As the life seeped out of Dylan's body, she strolled over to her comfy little sofa and wrapped the flowered sofa cover around her shoulders. She wondered if she could get a new one made out of the same material as her curtains.

They were such a good bargain.

******

F

One of the most powerful emotions we experience. We do this in varying degrees. There are those that run <u>to</u> the fire, and those that run <u>away</u> from it. Some people fear nothing, but I think privately, as complex as the human brain is, somewhere in the mess is a fearful synapse as yet activated. Snakes, bugs? I've seen some pretty nasty dudes scream at the sight of a thirsty scorpion.

Then there are the absolute craziest, meanest, most fearless killers alive, at least I hope they are. I am speaking about the armed forces of the United States, whom I maintain the utmost respect for. In my lifetime I have seen our soldiers idolized, hero-worshipped, and awarded. I have also seen returning soldiers castigated, mocked, and most embarrassing of all, ignored.

What's up with that? When the shit comes down, I want fire-breathing, testosterone-fueled maniacs manning the weapons with itchy trigger fingers. We can worry about the politics *after* the enemy is obliterated. Seems simple enough to me. The real trick is to not have to pick up weapons in the first place. To settle our differences using our God-given intelligence. Right.

Remember all citizens of planet Earth: we are all of us, similar physical beings floating on a rock in outer space. The only thing holding us to the rock is gravity and if this magnetic whatchamacallit just stops, so does the Carnival of Life. The end of the Carnival of Life? What a beautiful way to term death. I neither fear nor welcome it. The only real reason I don't want to die is because I don't want to take the chance of ever not seeing my beautiful soulmate Karen again. I'll need at least another lifetime to repay her.

At least that's what she keeps telling me.

Quit hurting each other.

Enjoy what time we are given.

Fear of the unknown is the theme of the next story *Amazon*.

The second story under this letter is one of the sickest so we'll just file it under freaky.

******

Amazon

Our guide was Tom Blevins, an absolute rock of a man. Forty years old, but his body looked more like it belonged to a man half his age. Not an ounce of visible body fat with huge, muscular arms and a khaki shirt that bulged with his massive chest as he shouted "There! On the port side! Hands inside the craft. Now!"

We were treated to a sight that is etched into my memory to this very day, some fifty-seven years later. The first hippo glided through the murky river water with its mouth wide open, revealing rows of uneven, discolored teeth which I had no doubt could have eaten me alive in one gulp. As the animal's mouth closed, he submerged, and little trails of air bubbles percolated from his flared gray nostrils. He seemed to float away from the tramp steamer, its eyes at half-mast. But he did not look sleepy to me. I was petrified, and my little fingers were clutched in a death-grip around my father's rough hand.

"It's OK son, he assured me. You're safe. Just do what the man says and you'll be fine."

No sooner had the first hippo appeared, than another equally massive, yet strangely graceful

Hippopotamus amphibius took its place and another and another. I got the panicky feeling they were closing in on our relatively small watercraft. I instinctively eased myself toward the bleached wooden bench in the center of our river boat. I was even more frightened as our guide fired two warning shots into the air to deter our guests from swimming any closer to us. I just *knew* I was going to die.

"No worries folks," Tom shouted above the trumpeting animals. "They are just singing."

Right, I thought. *Singing about their impending meal of a boatful of human flesh.*

"There on the port side! Can you see the tigers sunning themselves by the riverside?" Tom was pointing as I sat frozen in fear. Our fearless guide tried making what I'm sure he thought were amusing anecdotes, but I was not taking my eyes off the tigers languishing in the noon day sun. They definitely looked hungry to me.

As if reading my mind, or more precisely, my petrified stare, Tom assured me "No worries little mate, the tigers won't come out to us."

I didn't believe him for one second.

I couldn't have been more thankful as the boat winded away through the lush Amazon when I heard Tom give the orders

"Hands out of the water! Keep your arms and hands in the boat!"

A giant colorful snake of some sort twisted its massive body around an overhanging tree limb and flicked his blood-red tongue at us. I watched in silent terror as the hungry piranha approached us. I almost fell into unconsciousness as my father cradled me and the rest is just a blur until we approached the wooden dock. I had never been so relieved in my young life to reach land and as I looked back at what was now a lush, benign landscape with calm, green waters, I could hear:

"Thank you for joining us on the Jungle Cruise today folks, enjoy the rest of your day here at Disneyland, the Happiest Place on Earth."

******

G

Everyone is guilty.
It's just a matter of what.
Raise your hand if you throw out mailers for shopping and coupons. Raise your hand if you ever cursed (either out loud or to yourself) at some driver unknown to you. I used to be the world's worst driver. For some reason, and I do not know why or where I picked up the poor habit, but I used to be very proprietary of the roadway on which I was traveling. *Not in <u>MY</u> lane asshole!* To the point where you could not fit a single sheet of paper between my front bumper and the rear

bumper of the unfortunate person who happened to be driving in front of me. *Who's the asshole now?* Now, age, and several points against my driver's license later, have made me much more considerate and tolerant. The direction driving as an activity is taking is a little weird for me.

Driverless cars.

In a society where there is already little to NO accountability, this isn't exactly helping. I have no doubt they are already developing strategies in preparation of the impending wave of legal problems. By the time this book is printed (if ever), I am sure there will be an even crazier idea injected into the mainstream. Like flying cars. How awesome would that be?

Innocence is much easier to pull off than guilt. For innocence, if you truly *are* innocent, you don't have to do a thing. You don't have to *act* innocent; you either are or you are not. Doesn't it seem simple enough? How have the courts and government managed to bastardize the concepts of guilt and innocence to the point where no one believes there is such a thing as justice for all? Liberty? Freedom? Those concepts have never applied to the general population and I fear that it might never happen.

Yes, we are at liberty and free to color *within the lines* of this cartoon we call The United States of America.

******

Broken Light Bulb

Gina parked her car in the first row of spaces near the church entrance. It was an hour and a half until mass began, but she arrived early to confess her weekly sins. If ever she needed to go to confession, this was the week. She dipped her fingers into the holy water, made the sign of the cross, and then made her way to the confessional. Her low-heels clicked on the grey stone floor as she walked.

Click. Click. Click. Click.

She sat in a pew near the confessional compartments, pulled down the knee-rest, and began praying. She clutched her gold crucifix necklace tightly and silently mouthed her prayers of contrition. There were three others in line before her, but she needed the extra time anyway. It had been that kind of week.

Both outside compartments emptied at the same time. Gina saw it was a mother clutching her rosary with white knuckles. Her little girl, about the same size and age as Gina's nephew, stomped her shoes petulantly. The mother was mouthing her silent prayers while steering her daughter to the rows of candles, both lit and unlit. She slid two folded dollar bills into a slot, lit two candles, and knelt before the religious statue.

"Pray for Daddy baby," she instructed as her little girl lowered her head, asking for divine help in making Daddy better.

Gina entered the confessional and knelt; the priest obscured by the lattice window.

The sins began flowing: Bless me Heavenly Father for I have sinned. This is so hard to say. I was unfaithful to my spouse and had sex with another man…I stole money from one of the collection baskets…I drank alcohol to excess and….I improperly touched a young boy---my nephew.

Dead quiet.

After what seemed like hours, Gina broke the silence.

"Father?"

"Is there someone there? Yes child?"

"Father, Why are you telling me this? I thought **I** was supposed to confess to **you**."

******

H

Honesty is NOT the best policy.

It is the *only* policy. You can never go wrong telling the truth. It may cause financial loss, embarrassment, and loss of status, but you will keep your honor and by doing so, you honor your family and all those that came before you.

I told far too many lies in this lifetime, a fact I am none too proud of. You can be honest with yourself and dishonest to others and you are a liar and philosophically flawed. Or vice versa, and you give the *appearance* of being honest, which by my standard, is worse yet. A friend of mine in college once told me, "a lie is nothing, but the truth told backwards!" It must be nice to be able to compartmentalize like that. I was never any good at it. More like all-over-the-map type of focus.

How can you tell when a pathological liar is telling the truth? *You've got to believe me! I'm seriously telling the truth this time!* Think about it. I was raised to be honest, but far too often the little voice in my head was that of the tiny Hadite on my shoulder. The little red guy with the mini-trident seemed to have me figured out and which buttons to push to send me on another fruitless hedonistic sojourn. I knew I shouldn't listen, but the things he was telling me were so much more *fun* than the more intelligent alternatives. I have always taken my intelligence for granted, choosing to pull it out like an old plastic Christmas
wreath that goes on the outside of the front door every year. I used it as a way of ducking out of my assigned chores around the house when we were kids. I did my sister's ninth-grade homework (I was in fifth-grade), and they were the highest grades she ever received in high school.

Honest.

Restraint

It was a sunny Saturday afternoon, and I was taking advantage of the bank's extended weekend hours to transfer some funds and get some information on one of my accounts. After I parked, I passed a mother with three kids, each pulling her in different directions. I smiled. She returned it with a roll of her eyes and a half-smile which spoke volumes of her maternal instincts. She finished her ATM transaction, counting several twenties out, and herded her children into the red SUV. I smiled to myself and entered the bank.

There were two tellers, an elderly Latino woman and a young man who looked like he wasn't ready or able to shave the intermittent hairs sprouting from his acne-covered face. His clothes aspired to business casual and were in dire need of a good ironing. With fourteen obviously impatient customers to serve, I looked to see if the two shell-shocked employees had any help lingering in the wings. I decided to make my transactions online when I returned home, but I did want to speak with someone about the questions I had so I took a number from the plastic roller and sat down. I had just turned my phone on to surf the web and kill some time in anticipation of a lengthy wait, when a very energetic young blonde girl bounded up to me.

Extending her hand, she announced "Hi! I'm Gidget. How can I provide you with awesome customer service today?" I stood and offered my hand in return. She grabbed my hand and gave it a surprisingly strong squeeze and shake. I looked to the two lines, now containing at least ten customers each and asked,   "Is this a good time? I can wait a few minutes if you need me to."

"Oh, don't worry," she said. "Maria, you're OK, aren't you?"

Maria shot her a look that was unmistakable in its meaning. *Hell no, I'm not OK you fucking idiot, does it look like we're OK?* But Maria just uttered a soft "OK."

Now it was the customers' turn with the eye-rolling.

"See?" Gidget affirmed, "Everything is awesome! Right this way, we can sit in my office. Can I get you a water or coffee?" Her blue business suit did not have one wrinkle and her makeup looked like it was done professionally. She also looked to me to be about fourteen years old.

"No thanks, I'm good," I said. I shot another furtive glance toward the tellers as several customers decided they'd had enough and left through the fingerprint-smudged front door.

"Awesome!" Gidget exhorted, pointing to the chair in front of her desk. "The name on the account you are inquiring about sir?"

After providing my name, address, and phone number, I was greeted with a "perfect!" or "awesome!" after each answer. My exuberant Customer Service Specialist was really on top of her game today. I decided my information was neither perfect nor awesome but bit my lip as her phone rang.

I counted exactly nine "awesomes" in her brief conversation, and as she covered the phone receiver with her French nails, she whispered "Thank you for being so awesome and patient, I'll be right with you."

I smiled again and said to myself: *Really? Is awesome the only fucking word you learned in college? Not everything is awesome, and NOTHING is perfect. I hope your stupidity and lack of business acumen does not extend to teaching your children, that is if anyone was even more stupid or drunk enough to have sex with you. You just said it again. You've been on the phone exactly three minutes and you just said your tenth "awesome!" I cannot believe the idiots that run this bank even hired a fucking fool like you to represent them. Maybe, just maybe, if every one of your customers did not have a functioning brain and were twelve-year-olds, you might be considered "awesome" yourself. I, however, DO have a functioning brain and am NOT a twelve-year-old so fucking ENOUGH with the "awesome" already!*

Gidget truncated the phone call with her eleventh "awesome!" and smiled back at me. "Thank you so much for your patience and understanding Mark, how are you doing today?"

For just one millisecond I thought I had the perfect response, but then thought *No, that would be too easy.* Also captured in that split-second I could see my beloved mother's bony index finger wagging in my face. "There are no liars in this family *Markitos.*"

I looked to Gidget and smiled again.

"Awesome Gidget, how are you doing?"

******

I

Intriguing would probably fit every one of the stories in this compendium (I hope). However, I chose innocence, or more accurately, the end of innocence, as the subject. The following story chronicles the "official" end of my own chastity and recounts some of the best of a treasure trove of memories I carry from the kingdom of England.

I remember we stayed in an English country manor for a time just outside of Oxford near the River Thames. They had an immaculate putting green on site that I totally ruined. I completely flooded out another of the rooms when I left the hot water running all night. I basically did everything I possibly could to set back U.S.-Great

Britain relations by about fifty years. The Beatles were still evolving into the worldwide phenomenon they became, England ruled the world of football, winning the World Cup in 1966, and Alf Garnett laid the foundation for the racial policy of future U.S. president Donald Trump in the British sitcom *Till Death Us Do Part.*

I loved the food in England except I am not a big fan of lamb or mutton. Of the good: Bird's custard (yummy), fish and chips (must use Plaice caught from the North Atlantic), collecting Matchbox vehicle toys, the castles, the architecture, the museums, and the very best contribution the ancient country has ever given us---the miniskirt.

I was not so big on stinging nettles which sprang up in our garden from time to time. The other thing I was not so fond of was the racism the Brits showed toward others. They seemed to label anyone who was not white as a "wog." Blacks, Pakistanis, Indians, and anyone of color qualified for this denigration.

Now, before anyone wants to jump me for Brit-bashing, I have no doubt that this racism I witnessed was nothing approximating the same scale of violence and hatred at the same time that American citizens were suffering as we too, were continuing to learn what it means to be human.

******

The <u>Real</u> Summer of Love……Innocence

We lived in a small two-story house at the end of a shady country lane. There were three houses actually, all similarly constructed of dark brick. Our family thought the houses to be small, almost tiny, but they were considered to be quite large by British standards. The lane was bordered by tiny pink and purple flowers, hugged by a carpet of white moss.

The first house was occupied by a *very* British family and their *very* British son, Trevor. I remember trying to make an effort, at my mother's behest, to befriend the skinny, pasty-white, geeky little pain-in-the-ass. I went over to his house one day to see
if he wanted to go play some soccer, or rather more accurately, *football.*

"Soccer? Oh, you mean *football.*" He laughed as if he'd never heard the silly word. I wanted to strangle him. I would have to return.

I showed up right at the appointed hour of 4 pm. and was told to wait in the *parlor.* Trevor's mother tried to kill some time
by struggling at simple conversation while Trevor "readied" himself for play. Can you believe that? Readied himself for play? What kind of bullshit was that?

Trevor bounded down the staircase two steps at a time and was absolutely exuberant as he

bounced out the door and onto the large stone
porch. As it turned out, Trevor was an expert on
everything. I spent the next hour and a half acting
like I was having fun, but mainly putting up with
the little jerk was all I was doing. When I came
home for supper, Mom wanted to know how it
went.

"Great, we had a blast," I lied.

Mom smiled.

I never saw Trevor again.

In the third house lived Bobby and Sharon.
They were a young couple, probably in their mid-
twenties. Bobby was tall and fair, with the coolest
mutton chop sideburns, all blonde and bushy. I
secretly wished I had Bobby's mutton chop
sideburns.

Sharon, his wife, was the lust of my life. I
thought she was hot. *Red hot.* She was kind of
short, about 5'5" and a little bit chunky, but she
had the sexiest smile I had ever seen so far in my
young life. Every once in a while, as she was
flitting about the house or garden, I would sneak a
glimpse of her more-than-ample bosom staring at
me from behind her strained paisley top. How very
lucky was her infant baby, I used to think. I
secretly wished I had Bobby's wife.

It was the summer of my thirteenth year, and
I was determined to finally become a man. This
would be the summer.

The Summer of Love.

1967.

Tony was Sharon's little brother who lived on the other side of Aylesbury. He was my first British friend. I would meet up with Tony when he visited his sister, and together we would do chores for her while Bobby was at work in his stodgy, smoky office at the bank. After we were done, Sharon always tried to offer us money, and we always refused. We settled on an orange drink, but truth be known, we would have paid *her* if we had any real money of our own. The soda made my throat bite, right at the spot where my tongue stops and my throat begins.

Life was good.

Tony and I had a blast that summer, running for miles along the banks of the Thames River. Sometimes we would end up in another town or village and find someplace to buy sweets. It was a glorious summer playing along the locks in the canal jetties, the dark hulls of the dank boats nearly invisible as they blended into the black waters of the Thames. We took great comfort playing and running along the river as we always knew our way home.

Tony was from a very modest family that lived across town. Theirs was one of the small box houses so tightly crammed together that they looked like the middle houses were going to collapse under the pressure from the outer homes. The thing I remember most about Tony's house was the smells. On the rare occasion I found myself in Tony's kitchen in the morning, it was the smoky assault of fried kippers, a small, tasty fish popular for breakfast (with eggs, of course!). The smell, rich and hearty, permeated the entire house. You could even detect it in the *loo* upstairs. I was also quite taken with the smell of fresh milk, right out of the bottle. His mom would use one of her shiny silver butter knives to poke through the top two or three inches of rich cream and butterfat. The milk we drink now resembles none of the above.

Somehow, that wonderful summer, my attention changed direction from lusting after Sharon, to lusting after Brittany.

Brittany was Sharon's babysitter and every thirteen-year-old sex maniac's dream. She was sixteen, a veritable *expert* on sex, and she wore the hottest fashion of the times: mini-skirts. Actually, hers were more like mini-mini-skirts.

I was in heaven.

Brittany dated older boys; blokes with cars and jobs and the lot, so I knew it would take some work on my part to make it happen. I figured I had all summer.

The hard part was getting past the watchful eye of my mother. I had overheard my parents' hushed conversations about
how "that girl is too sexy" and other remarks about Brittany, and they were all true. She even had the added excitement to me of smoking pot. Like I said every thirteen-year-old sex maniac's dream.

Every Friday night, she would show up at Bobby and Sharon's, and for the first month my mom had managed to find a way for me to NOT get together with Brittany. As oversexed as I was, I drew upon a fierce resolve and remained undaunted.

On the very next Friday night, it finally happened.

My mom and dad were entertaining, and our house was full of good cheer and about a dozen of my parents' friends. I got lucky. Probably the *only* thing that could draw my mom's attention away from her oversexed teenage boy's intentions was entertaining a group of people. Any amount, any occasion. The consummate hostess.

Brittany would be arriving exactly at seven in her mini-mini skirt, and I was about to make my way to the entrance of the lane to walk her to Bobby and Sharon's. I was like a loyal puppy dog, now that I look back at it.

After our usual chit-chat, I left Brittany on the porch and said, as I did every Friday night, that I would try to see her later. She reached out and touched my arm. She was close enough I could smell the liquor on her breath. An electric shock was coursing through my body. I can still remember how it felt that day. She looked at me with her cat-like green eyes, caked heavily with mascara. "I *really* hope you can come over tonight," she slurred.

Now, I am not one to make guarantees, other than that I will be sleeping next to my wife at evenings end. However, I *guarantee* you I was not going to miss out on that opportunity. I knew that neither hell nor high water would be keeping me away from Brittany that evening.

I returned to my house and did my best to be in the way of everyone at the party. After about a half an hour I waited for my chance. Mom was surrounded by five or six people. As she glanced my way, she stopped talking about the room decorations and asked "Need something Markitos?

"May I please go over and see my friend to watch TV?"

An innocent-enough question, but now with ten pair of eyes focused on her reaction, she was none too appreciative of the timing. She relayed that information silently, with that look only a mother can give her son when she knows she just got had. I still remember her dark eyes looking directly into mine.

"Have a good time," she relented in a cloud of cigarette smoke.

"Okay, thanks mom." I kissed her on the cheek, and I was *gone*.

I cleared the hedge that bordered our houses within about three seconds. I was ringing the doorbell and trying to look as cool as a thirteen-year-old sex maniac could.

Brittany answered the door and it was on.

You would think that such a watershed moment in my personal story would be indelibly ingrained in my memory, that I would recall every last little detail, but the truth is I remember very little of that night. I suppose I was in such a big hurry to become a "man," that the boy remaining in me forgot to remember anything. I suppose I did alright; at least the "expert" Brittany said so. The British are very polite, remember, so…I didn't set any world records or anything, but the deed was indeed done.

I never saw Brittany again after leaving England several years later.

Because of the incessant rainy seasons, there is a joke among the locals who dwell in the Midlands, that area in central England south of London and north of Cornwall, that "summer falls on a Friday."

I still believe that.

******

J

.positionJuxta I just invented this. I don't know why it is funny; I just know it is.

Jaded is a term I first remember being used as a descriptor for the world's greatest rock-n-roll band, The Rolling Stones led by the ultimate Jaders—who also happen to be two of the greatest songwriters in music history---Mick Jagger and Keith Richards. I am a little confused about this one, though. While I think it is cool to try just about everything there is to experience, I still think that there are *some* things that are better imagined than experienced. I still enjoy getting high, but if someone told me that I could get *really* high if I set off a firecracker in my butt while I took a hit, well, not even I will fall for that one again.

I include two stories under this emotion, one-story set-in Sin City, and the other on a sunny Sunday morning in Greece.

Jaded covers a lot of territory. Where on the sick continuum does jaded lie? Is it closer to deviant or maybe a little more akin to twisted? I like to think that all of my rock star heroes are jaded. Ditto that for actors and actresses, singers and songwriters. You can even extend that to painters and artists. What they do is every bit as unfathomable to me as Houdini or David Copperfield. I don't know how many canvasses I tried painting along with Bob Ross only to discover that as a painter, I'm an OK writer.

Now my athlete-heroes are another story.

Given that the average NFL career for an elite athlete is just over three years, all I ask is that the starting running back on my favorite team can just *wait* to finish their playing career and then enjoy everything this planet has to offer. Seems reasonable enough. One thing that makes me wonder is that this all-too-brief career longevity is *today*, with all the technology and protections in place for players.

Rules are slowly catching up and I am sure the entire NFL will breathe a little easier when the last of the bashed-in-brain-boys of the league die off, reducing the potential amount of their long-overdue awards.

Man, it doesn't take much to get me started, does it?

Beauty……Jaded

It was another Friday night in Las Vegas, and I was looking to fall in love.

My third girlfriend in as many months had given me my pink slip and I was tiring of the Strip prostitutes with whom I had become far too familiar. I decided to try my luck at the poker room of the Strip casinos. They had just hired a poker icon, a multiple winner of Binion's Horseshoe Casino World Poker Championship, to serve as Poker Room Manager. I sat down at the seven-card stud table and promptly went on a hot streak, amassing several large stacks of green twenty-five-dollar chips. I was up about sixteen-hundred when I abruptly sat down from the table and wandered over to the five-card draw table where my good luck continued.

I was a typical gambler. I would go out and win a lot of money, only to lose it back that same evening. However, as long as the hot streak lasted, I was the King. I would buy bottles of Dom for every player at my table when I was hot and once tipped a busty cocktail waitress a black chip (one hundred dollars) for bending over in front of me. She had just dropped off my champagne, and I "accidentally" threw the chip on the floor at the girl's feet. When she looked to me, I told her the chip was hers if she would give me a peek at the goods. She looked at me like I was some sort of bug that had smashed into her windshield. Then, she obviously thought about it, spun around, and bent down to pick up the token. She stayed there for about five full seconds, turned her head to me and asked.

"You good, George?" She was sarcastically flattering me with the moniker given to big tippers in the glitzy city in the desert.

"All yours, girl."

She picked up her tip, tucked it into her bra, and gave me the smashed-bug-look again before resuming her rounds through the casino.

The King.

I lost back a lot of money but ended the night almost eight hundred to the good. I went upstairs to the bar overlooking the live circus acts and ordered a triple V.O. and a Heineken chaser.

Then I saw her.

At the other end of the bar, the most beautiful woman I had ever seen was talking and laughing loudly. She was obviously over her limit, and I was mesmerized as she climbed off her bar stool and jumped up on top of the bar. She stood there in her low-cut blouse, exposing a perfect pair of breasts.

"Would you care for some company?" I asked as I walked on over.

"Sure, good-lookin' park it."

She had amazing violet eyes, reminding me of Liz Taylor's. Her eyelashes were long and curled, and her hair was auburn, matching her glittering lipstick. Her skirt was super-short, and I have yet to see another pair of legs as finely shaped as hers. She had perfectly mani-pedi French nails, the color an exact match to the hair and lipstick. She also had a butterfly tattoo on her left ankle. Her skin was like Devonshire cream, all buttery and soft. It was apparent that she was very well cared for. Her smile exposed beautiful white teeth usually reserved for the rich or entertainers.

She climbed back down from the bar and we talked for almost an hour. She was at once beautiful, sexy, smart, and the type of woman who is only alone when she wants to be.

All of this and only thirty-three inches tall. WTF?

******

Fish Tale

The early morning mist lying low over the lake was a majesty to behold, as the sun fought to spray its pink and yellow streaks across the summer sky. Theo cast his line into the water and began the tease. The shiny red lure worked like a charm, enticing the first fish of the day to bite. He pulled his pole back and up in one motion, firmly hooking his catch. It was going to be a great day. The next five hours were spent alternating between casting his line, reeling in fish, and taking swigs from his flask of Ouzo.

It was approaching high noon, the sun reflecting off the water like a thousand gold drachmas. Lake Volvi had produced a basket of plump perch and Theo called for his sons.

"Dimitri! Hermes! Come!" he shouted. The boys came tearing over the rocky hill. "Slow down," he ordered, but it was too late for Hermes as he tumbled over the rocks and into the cool water. He pulled himself up, wiping at the blood on his knee.

"You see? I told you to slow down," Theo lectured, wrapping a rag around the little boy's leg. He knew it was no use; boys are going to run around lakes and fathers are going to lecture. *As it has been for thousands of years*, Theo said to himself.

"Did you catch many fish Papa?" Dimitri asked.

"Yes, my son. It has been a fruitful day. We must leave now; we will be late for dinner."

"You boys each take a handle of the cooler and follow me," Theo barked. Dimitri and Hermes each lifted their skinny little arms, barely keeping the cooler from dragging across the rocks.

Theo was holding up a huge carp and a stringer full of yellow perch. He was grinning from ear to ear as a stranger stopped.

"Wow that is some catch! The fish gods must have been with you," the stranger remarked.

"Yes it was a blessed day indeed," Theo replied.

"What's in the cooler?" the stranger asked.

"Just the babies. Thank you for the kind words and be well sir," Theo said in parting. He shouted to the boys.

""Don't you *dare* drop that cooler! Stop and rest every so often if you must," Theo barked at his sons, obviously struggling under the weight.

As they ascended the hill and approached the truck, another man shouted his admiration for the bounty of fish Theo was holding aloft.

"More big fish in the cooler?" he asked.

"Naw, just little ones," Theo answered.

As the boys tried to hoist the cooler up onto the tailgate of the truck, Hermes fell off balance, dropping his end of the cooler. It tumbled open, a stew of blood, little human arms, legs, and skulls spilling over the grassy rocks.

The stranger screamed. "Oh God, what have you done you monster!"

"Told you I had the little ones in there," Theo grinned.

******

K

Kindness is such a basic requirement for membership in the human race that it is almost an embarrassment to list it.

"It doesn't cost anything to be clean or respectful."

A mom-ism that is an untenable low benchmark for how one purports oneself. I'll add that it also does not cost a cent to be polite, approachable, or even (gasp!) friendly.

Oh, we always hear stories of kindness around the holidays and we always ask, "why can't people do nice things like that all year long?" I personally enjoy the *feeling* of Christmas every bit, if not more than the holiday itself. One of the main reasons we choose (yes my wife has once again enabled my insanity) to keep Christmas lights up in our front room all year long. I'm a total sucker for Christmas movies. Anything with a dog (that doesn't die), anything with orphans, the elderly, or the hopeless, I will watch and smart money says I'll be crying like a baby before it is all over. That is why it <u>absolutely makes me sick</u> that someone chose to desecrate the single most personally-treasured holiday on this entire planet. Universally celebrated in some fashion or another and held closest to the little hearts of children. They still see the world as a place of wonder and magical possibilities. You can take shots at the Easter Bunny (no pun intended), you can *really* have a Turkey Shoot, but you *leave Christmas alone!* I speak of the proliferation of Santa slasher movies that began after 1984's *Silent Night, Deadly Night.* He is the first writer I remember who used the quill to burst the collective bubbles of all of us waiting for St. Nicholas on Christmas Eve. By doing so, he has irreversibly destroyed an institution that was meant to last for all time. He had no human right to impinge unholy images into our children's hopeful bright eyes. In the process he stained what is arguably the very best day of each year we are fortunate to be alive for. The unselfishness to cause such irrevocable damage to the Holiest of days is absolutely unforgivable.

I wish I had thought of it.

******

"Junior! Junior!" his mother yelled from the kitchen. She was hovering over a tray of homemade meatballs pulled hot from the oven. They smelled of garlic and oregano and Junior was hungry. Really hungry.

"I can hear Billy crying again. Can you please go see if his diaper needs changing?"

"Aw mom," Junior protested.

The extended index finger emphasized his mother's threatening tone.

"Not one word. You promised me if I got you a car, you would help make up the cost by helping me with Billy. Besides, we really couldn't afford Maria anyway. It's only for a few more months. With your help, I'll be able to quit the night job soon."

"Alright, alright." Junior knew the futility of trying to win an argument with his mother, *especially when she was right*. He trudged down the dark, narrow hallway and carefully approached Billy's room.

"Oh shit!" Junior screamed. "Mom! I'm gonna throw up! There's poop everywhere!"

"Plenty of nose pins on the laundry line", she offered. "Here, smear some of this under your nose," as she tossed him the little blue jar of Vapo-Rub.

"Oh man. Stop crying." *Jesus he cries all the time.* Junior approached the screaming, helpless little body. He wiped his bare back of the dried feces and carefully turned him over. Billy stopped screaming and settled into a muffled sob. Junior used another towel to clean the rest of Billy's body. He knew that a mess this big was gonna have to be cleaned up and a bath given. He removed the soiled diaper like he was defusing a neutron bomb.

Almost telepathically, his mother bellowed from the kitchen.

"Junior, how is he? After you clean him up, you get some bleach-water towels to sanitize the room. I mean the *whole* room. Then……"

"I know, I know. A bath."

"Thank you. You're such a good boy."

His mother returned to kneading the little pasta-potato pillows for her gnocchi primavera.

Junior spent the next half-hour cleaning up Billy's entire room.

How the fuck do you get shit on the walls? I didn't think your skinny little arms could throw that far.

Junior was speaking into Billy's vacant eyes. As he lifted the tiny body, Junior had to say something, but he just couldn't bring himself to call him by his name--- *Billy*.

"It's OK Grandpa, I'll take care of you."

******

L

"Love makes the world go 'round, but money greases the wheels."

A brother-ism this time that I am sure, like all good sayings, is stolen. With apologies to Darry Strawberry, "it is money that is the straw that stirs the drink." The facts are undeniable. If you have the wherewithal to read these words, take a second to remember all those fellow Earth-mates that do not enjoy what would amount to a real luxury in their lives. The ability to access and read. To learn. What a better world the entire Sphere of Life would be if the education level of every one of its inhabitants was raised? I suppose it is just too difficult a task to ask of our legislators to use a holistic lens to guide their course of actions rather than the fractured *lens obscura* through which the only things that are clearly visible to them are precincts, polls, and percentages.

Two words that should never be used in the same room are budget and education. Since I am presuming a certain level of education from our nation's leaders and shapers of policies, they must see the terms as antithetical. To make it easier for them to understand, just replace the word "Budget" with "Limit" and then let them explain to their own children that the sky is not the limit; it is actually lower due to budget considerations. Right?

Perspective.

But back to love. I love everything about love. I love the feeling people have, the glow they get, and the emotional responses it elicits. I never used to know the true meaning of the words "I love you."

You remember that feeling you had when you met the very first boyfriend or girlfriend you ever had? Think back to when you wrote their name on everything. The need to see them early in the morning before school, then during breaks from class, skipped classes, and after school. Once home, you were on the phone to them making plans to meet later that night, or at the very *latest* tomorrow morning before school. Remember how you thought you physically ached because you weren't together?

Approaching forty years plus of marriage, I still feel that way about my wife Karen.

******

Another Love Story

Day One

It was a cool October morning, and I parked, grabbed my lunchbox, and headed toward good 'ol

Building 66. As I approached the entrance, a blue Toyota came bouncing off the speed bumps, Axl Rose and Guns–n-Roses blaring from some seriously amped-up speakers. The driver swerved and almost hit me, without even looking. She parked in the carpool lane. No one else was in the car. Oh well, I thought.

She stepped out of the car, and it was all over but the shouting. I was in love!

As we approached the elevator, I waited for her to board, but she stopped and held the vibrating cell phone to her ear. Holding out her hand in a gesture meant to say, "hold on for a sec," I waited patiently and stepped aside for another co-worker to board. She was literally shouting into the little speaker. After listening to an embarrassing conversation that frankly was not the most appropriate for a job setting, one of the passengers in the now half-full elevator pressed our floor button. She slipped in at the very last second before the doors closed.

Oh well, I thought.

I didn't see her again until lunch. As I arrived at the corridor leading to the break room, the unmistakable odor of burning popcorn permeated everything. As I entered the kitchen, there she was, draining the last drop out of the last pot of coffee. I watched intently (told you I was in love!) as she placed the empty pot back on the hot burner.

"That will burn if you leave it there," I offered.

"First the popcorn, then this," she replied.

After introducing myself, I proceeded to tell Bunny the process of how to make more coffee. She was obviously

disinterested. She was a new employee, and I shared with her my understanding of the culture and work environment. I hoped she   would adjust quickly. I said goodbye and could not get her off of my mind.

Day Two

As I entered the parking lot, I saw the blue Toyota and looked for her. She was standing at the building entrance with one foot holding the door open while she furiously worked at extracting the last bit of nicotine from her cigarette. She tossed her smoldering butt in the general direction of the ashtray, the ashes exploding as it hit the ground. Several employees fanning away the second-hand smoke looked on in disdain.

"What did you bring for lunch today?" I asked.

"Salmon and broccoli today," she answered.

"Something was really good in the fridge yesterday!"

"What do you mean?" I asked.

"Whoever brought in the stuff in the blue container in the first fridge. Delicious."

I wanted to explain how it is not polite or civilized to steal food from someone else but instead smiled and stirred my coffee. We headed to our respective cubes after a nice chat. After agreeing to meet later, I walked her to the door. She was walking so slowly, I self-consciously stepped aside to let the crowd forming behind us pass at a normal pace. She was unfazed by this.

"People are sure in a hurry around here", she observed.

Of course they are in a hurry! This is a business! A place where work is performed! That is the process for how business gets done! Moving at a reasonable pace is a <u>highly desired</u> activity! That was what I instinctively wanted to say, but all that came out was "yeah," (in love!).

We agreed to meet for dinner.

Day Three

At 10 am on Wednesday morning I was greeted by the face I had seen so many times in my dreams since Monday. I was on the phone with a client and in the middle of my reply, Bunny cut in.

"Hi. You busy?" she asked.

Of course I am busy! Can't you see that I am on the phone? Do you have any concept of politeness or professionalism? When someone is talking on the phone, it is quiet time! Time to SHUT THE FUCK UP!

That was what I instinctively wanted to say, but what came out was "never too busy for you" (love!).

Bunny's cell rang loudly. She began a conversation so loud and obtrusive that several nearby employees grimaced. As she finished her conversation, it was obvious that I would remain on the phone for quite a while longer. She stood impatiently it seemed, as I continued my call. Saying nothing, just *standing* there. Talk about annoying. I shrugged my shoulders, muted my headphone and arranged to meet her later that evening for dinner. As she departed my cube, I detected an odor that was neither pleasant nor associated with the Chinese food being enjoyed by my assistant.

Oh well, I thought (love!).

Day Four

Pouring my early morning cup of java, I detected the odor of a burning coffee pot. We were the only two people in the break room. We were the only two people in the *world* as far as I was concerned! I was going to take Bunny to lunch at noon, and she met me at my cubicle promptly at 12:15. I had taken a call, not knowing if our date was still on or not, so I pointed to my headset as she approached. She listened for a minute and before I could speak, she blurted "I know what they are asking for. The same thing happened to me!"

I quickly muted my headset and smiled (love!). That was definitely **not** my instinctive reaction.

I was on my way home at the end of my shift when I could see Bunny sitting at another employee's desk. I waved goodbye, as I was cutting it close to be at a doctor's appointment I had specially arranged for.

"Leaving without saying goodbye?" she asked.

I apologized and explained my doctor's appointment. She went on and on about her day and what she was thinking we could do this weekend. I glanced furtively at my watch and could not be more obvious that I was in a hurry. On she went. I finally had reached the very limit of my time.

"I will see you tonight," I said.

Tonight? I told you I was going out," she protested.

"In my dreams, Bunny."

I smiled and left.

Day Five

I couldn't eat. I couldn't sleep. All I could think about was this new employee and how I couldn't live without her. I drove in to work with a real sense of urgency and knew what I had to do and say. I had rehearsed it all night and all morning in preparation. I saw Bunny sitting at the bench by the parking garage as three fat little birds danced in the shade. I slid next to her, put my arm around her, and proceeded to explain how I felt and how I absolutely could not live without her. When I was done, I turned her shoulders square to me and gazed deeply into her eyes.

"Will you marry me?" I asked.

"Yes, yes, yes!" she blurted, showering me with kisses.

"I have only one request of you Bunny," I continued.

"What is it? Anything! Anything for you!" she laughed.

"You need to get another job."

******

M

There is nothing more terrifying as a heinous act committed by someone totally insane and out of control (and I'm not referring to married life).

In my lifetime I saw the press cover the horrific Charles Manson murders, making it tough to tell who the bloodsuckers and suckees were. No reason whatsoever for the last sentence except it felt cool to type it. Just when I thought I had seen it all, Jeffrey Dahmer comes along and ruins my appetite.

Madness.

Not to say all madness is this severe. For example, it was truly horrific and absolute *madness* when the skinny young weather girl on the local news wore black and white! Stripes! Can you imagine? And that hair. What *was* she thinking?

Madness.

I actually worked, as a high school senior, at a state mental institution. I earned extra credit for my Psychology class. On Saturdays I would assist with handing out prescriptions and general helping out for six patients. I talked with them, watched TV, read with them and to them, and walked around the *campus*. I even go to hang out in their own version of a teen club where we would spin records. We talked about the same type of things, listened to a lot of the same music, even played some sports (wicked good ping pong players). We were dressed similarly and I never once noticed anything different about them. They seemed to be as normal as I am.

Wait a second…

I cast a wide net with the second emotion, Maternal. I figured anyone who has a mom will be able to relate so I can't go wrong right? We'll see.

They say there is no greater love than a mother has for her child, and I believe it. My own mom left this world far too soon. I miss her every day.

I actually have another draft for a story that I considered *too sick* to ask to have published. I love the stories where a mother of
one species takes over the care and nurturing of an infant from a different species. How is that not cool? The human child birthing thing?

No.

Next subject.

******

School's Out

Detective Matt Kennedy got off the elevator on the 6th floor. The shiny doors parted to reveal a pile of seven bodies. Blood pooled from the underside of several overturned corpses. A head, or rather, the fragments of brain and bone that once *were* a head, remained hanging precipitously by what appeared to be a neck. It gave no indication of identity. The coppery smell of death permeated the entire floor. As he gently tiptoed his way over bodies, the shredded remnants of the windpipe of a young woman tangled itself around his left ankle. He vomited twice, searching out a dry patch of carpet to deposit the Big Mac he ate ten minutes ago. Matt looked in every direction, greeted by the most horrific crime scene he had ever witnessed in his 23-year career in the Phoenix Police Department. The walls were splattered with different hues of blood red, purple, black bile, and some stains that could not be found in *any* color spectrum.

"Matt?"

He turned to the elevator, a Pavlovian response to the *gong* of the elevator announcing its arrival. It was his partner, Jimmy Reese, all 24 years of him.

"Jimmy, what the hell happened here?" Matt asked incredulously. He could tell his young partner was falling apart.

"It's like this on every floor! All seven of them! Bodies, blood, all dead. The Crime Scene Unit is sending three teams, should be arriving soon." Jimmy looked to his hero Matt for strength. Jimmy was six-foot five, weighed 275 lbs. and had played football for the Sun Devils before missing his shot with a severed Achilles tendon injury. At this very moment he was as weak as a newborn.

"Easy, Big Dogg," Matt offered. The wailing of an entire squadron of police vehicles pierced through the walls and alerted the detectives to return to the first floor. They carefully made their way back to the elevators, traversing the other side of the building but finding more of the same madness. What looked like a human organ of some kind; a liver or something vital, blocked his path to the linoleum. As Jimmy delicately lifted his foot, he felt his right foot giving way to the slippery body fluids congealing under his weight. The enormous man fell face first, into what remained of a human corpse's stomach. Jimmy shrieked, drawing Matt near, already removing his windbreaker to offer Jimmy. Not one word was spoken.   The men silently entered the elevator, pushing the blood-streaked floor button for "1."

As the detectives made their way to the front doors, Jimmy turned to Matt.

"Can you believe this happened here, of all places? I got my *degree* from this online university!" Jimmy shouted at no one in particular. I can't believe it! I just can't believe it!" Jimmy was hysterical now. "I can't believe it."

"I can't believe it! I did it again. I overslept again!" Julie sighed and rolled over on her side. Now THAT was a dream! I better get going. Don't wanna be late for work at good 'ol Online U."

******

Life……Maternal

"Push! Push! Come on Nan, you can do it! Almost there now. Push!" her husband John cried out.

Nancy gritted her teeth one more time and shoved. She already had two babies, both delivered by C-section. But *this* was *real* pain. This required physical exertion like nothing she'd ever had to do in her life. Add in the fact that she was approaching her fortieth birthday soon and was not in the best of shape anyway.

She felt like the ugliest monster on the face of the earth as she grunted and pushed with all her might. She just didn't have the strength she had when she was twenty and giving birth to her first daughter.

"Push Nan Push!" John shouted.

Her face contorted and Nancy could feel John's arm around her shoulder as…

"One more time!" he shouted and the weight was suddenly lifted.

The unconscious body of her mother tumbled awkwardly over the cliff, crushing her skull and scattering blood, bone, and other vital fluids on the rocky coast.

"Damn, she was heavy," Nancy grunted to John as she fired up a joint. She took a deep hit and handed it to him.

"And I thought having kids was hard."

******

N

Narcissistic. Naughty. Instead of these salacious emotions, I went with Needy. If you've

ever needed something to the point that it is no longer a want you may relate to the couple in the next story. I don't consider myself a needy person. At least my needs are simple. I think everyone's needs are simple. Oxygen, water, food, and shelter. Boom. OK, maybe throw in a job. A pet. Anything else falls in the want category. The disparity lies in how the needs are fulfilled. I must be truly great for me to have decided all this for the human race! I tell Karen all the time that when I am over everything (in charge of everything in the world) I will be making some changes. I will be the only person on the planet with access to the internet. No cell phones. No people driving 45 miles-per-hour in the high-speed lane, no meanness, re-instatement of the Code of Hammurabi, no semi-trucks allowed on ANY freeway while I am using it, no pollution, no commercials, no airline oligarchy, free health care, free education, salary based on
contribution to the whole, and finally, pay-for-performance for *every* elected politician. You know, the more I read my own lines the more convinced I am that something is seriously wrong with me.

Take a subject such as college football, for example. I have always been a Notre Dame fan. My father used to tell me at his school, the nuns (Sisters of the Holy Cross) would march he and his four brothers into school playing the Notre Dame

Victory March. The song is one of the most recognizable college football
fight songs ever. Now, with that being said, I *want* the Fighting Irish to win another national championship, but first I *need* someone to find a way to stop Alabama, Ohio State, USC, and the others. Right?

My impartial take is simply *everyone* is a Notre Dame fan, some just refuse to admit it. In the Final Walk up to the pearly gates of heaven, those standing in line as they approach St. Peter will undergo a slight metamorphosis. Forget "On Wisconsin," "Hail to the Victors," and "Fight On." Inching closer to FINAL ADMITTANCE through the gates (and I have NO doubts about this) EVERYONE will start humming the Notre Dame Victory March.

Just in case…

******

Powerless

Sean Keaton is madly in love with Kelly O'Hara. How does he know? How will he ever know?

He knows because he curses the days, hours, even minutes that they are apart. He knows because he physically aches for her touch. Her elegant neck simply adorned with an emerald necklace; her green eyes dancing as her crimson curls laugh around her soft white shoulders. Yes, Sean Keaton is very much in love. He could hardly wait to see her tonight.

Kelly O'Hara is madly in love with Sean Keaton. No questions here. Kelly has lived within two blocks of Sean her entire life, all twenty-two years of it. She doesn't exactly remember when it happened, only that it did happen, and she has loved Sean deeply for as long as she can remember. She was flooded with excitement and anticipation of seeing her love tonight.

Their eyes met and the entire world melted away.

She moved with the sexual power and grace of a predatory feline. Sean was mesmerized. As Kelly glided ever closer, Sean extended his hand. Kelly clasped it and placed it gently, lovingly, on her heaving chest. Their eyes locked in a knowing gaze and Sean could feel Kelly's sweet, warm breath as her pulled her closer.

Kelly was wearing a dark-blue Armani power suit that puddled on the floor. Both lovers worked frantically trying to undress each other. Time stood still amidst a flurry of torn silk, ripped buttons, and exposed flesh. Kelly ripped the snug t-shirt off Sean's tight pecs, exposing his six-pack abs and eliciting an appreciative sigh from Kelly.

Her eyes widened in excitement. She raked her long French nails across his rippled muscles.

The two stood before each other, fully exposed and fully in love beyond words. Sean's eager, hot lips parted Kelly's, and he tenderly explored her mouth with his silky tongue. He furiously grabbed her backside with both of his large hands. He pulled her tighter. Closer…

Kelly was absolutely incendiary. She reached for the hardest part of Sean and slowly knelt before him. Sean's eyes rolled as he gasped out Kelly's name. *Oh Kelly, Kelly, Kelly….*

Kelly rose, winked at Sean, and smiled.

Sean could wait no longer. He lifted Kelly, inserted himself, and began rocking her in a rhythmic, animalistic dance. Their sweaty bodies climaxed simultaneously as trains collided, surf crashed to shore, and Sean and Kelly consummated their undying love.

As the two lovers dressed, Sean peered around the corner, catching the eye of a pretty young blonde.

"Waitress, Sean said. I think we're ready to order now"

I love coming to this restaurant.

******

O

Optimism.

Half-empty or half-full?

I am a half-full guy, often avoiding the unavoidable in my lifelong pursuit of trying to find good in every person. I am now willing to admit that it is not gonna happen. Some people are just assholes.

'Hope for the best but expect the worst."

If ever there was a total bullshit saying, this is it. Let me reiterate. We are all only here for a brief life span. ALWAYS hope for the best and EXPECT the best. It will make the brief stay here more enjoyable, believe me. And when your hopes are fulfilled, it is that much sweeter of an accomplishment because you *knew* it would happen. Do not try to avoid disappointment, it is just another mandatory emotion to round out the body of text that is the human experience. To be disappointed just means that you were in a position to achieve, rather than being a mere spectator.

I had a friend in South Carolina who was a pessimist. He was down on absolutely everything on earth. He loathed others who were not of his same narrow mind. Chicken Little was the Ultimate Optimist to hear Randy's version. The weather, no matter how beautiful and temperate currently, would soon enough turn horrible and probably life-threatening. Any girl he met was out to ruin his life (if that was even possible). If war, pestilence, or crime did not erase man from planet earth, something else terrible and most certainly painful, would. He thought we were being "programmed" at a time when computers were the size of an SUV and there were exactly <u>two</u> computer languages. Two. BASIC and COBOL.

Millennials Google it.

The pessimist won't go anywhere because something bad might happen. It could be too dangerous or requires more effort than they want to give. They won't try a new dish (poison), God forbid get on an airplane (crash), climb a mountain (avalanche), or go to school (sniper).

That school sniper thing is courtesy of the 21st century.

What the hell is wrong with us?

******

Sunset……Optimistic

I met Sheila on a beach on Key Largo, and the sunset was an orange-pink starburst as we splashed in the clear emerald waters. The palm trees stood sentry to our passionate love-making as night, with its dark blues and purples, fought to take hold. I looked deep into her eyes and have not found my way back ever since. We interlocked our fingers and walked for hours, talking about well, *everything.* She expounded on theories, commented on international politics, and could recite the last twenty winners of the Heisman Trophy, annually awarded to the nation's best college football player. She was absolutely beautiful, more beautiful than any girl I had ever seen. Her auburn hair reflected the intruding silver moonbeams as the sun ducked for cover under the horizon.

Intelligent, we could and did, speak on every subject imaginable. The lush tropical landscape was dotted and splashed with a palette of bright colors and their perfume danced lightly in the intermittent winds. When she laughed, it came from the belly, and it was infectious. The week we spent there was the most miraculous of my life. I have never met any girl who so quickly owned my very soul and with such little effort. Our respective vacations were nearing their *denouements*, and we decided to continue our relationship when we both returned to civilization.

Three short months later, I am far-removed from the Florida Keys, carefully stepping over a small puddle in Minot, North Dakota. The wind is blowing steadily, but at least the rain has stopped. I look at the permasludge gray snow piled up on the sidewalks and leaking into the sewer drains. I roll my eyes and say to myself *Key Largo this is not.* Just saying the words takes me back to the white sandy beaches and the walks with Sheila. I can smell flowers, lots of sweet-smelling tropical flowers.

But something is wrong.

I know I fell head over heels for Sheila, but what did I really know about her? Would she maintain her perfect figure? And if so, for how long? Her mother is corpulent, and so is her father. Would she be genetically disposed to life as a fat woman? She really portrayed herself as athletically inclined, and she was certainly athletically knowledgeable. But would she change in midstream and suddenly lose interest in sports?

I am a sports nut, a true sports fanatic. I really hope this does not become a problem. Last night she drank more wine than I ever could. Is she an alcoholic, or does she have a drinking problem? My head was spinning as all these thought bombarded me. She suddenly seems shorter than I remembered and I can't tell, but it looks like Sheila is slightly club-footed. Genetic?

More thoughts intruded. Is she really the one? A possible bride for me? I certainly can't imagine marrying anyone who was not a sports nut like me. I'm not a nerd, by any means, but I can't imagine going out drinking all the time either.

I mean, vacation was one thing, but I really couldn't hang with a lush. I can't be certain, but I thought I detected a severe case of halitosis when Sheila was singing along with a car commercial. I *hate* singing along with commercials.

Lame.

Suddenly, I am walking along the beach at Coral Reef State Park, my fingers intertwined with

Sheila's. Of course, it was yet another magical sunset. I look at her quizzically as she squeezes my hand tighter and tighter. Tighter.

"Hey! What are…"

Sheila was staring at me, her eyes like lasers. I leaned in closely as she spoke.

"Michael, are you going to say it? Quit embarrassing me!"

"I do. I do," I stammered, as the church echoed with nervous laughter.

"I now pronounce you man and wife. You may kiss the bride," the priest proclaimed.

******

P

It seems logical to think under this letter I would go from optimism to pessimism.

Nope.

Another P word that is fun is Ptolemaic. I just don't know enough about Ptolemy or the intricacies of his system of astronomy to comment. Parsimonious is a rhythmic descriptor but when was the last time someone told you, "Don't be parsimonious, leave a tip"? It usually comes out like "You cheap bastard, don't be a fucking idiot!"

Not that you can accuse me of being a tightwad by any means. I will always over-tip for average service. I have great empathy for the food service workers, so I have few minimal requests:

- Acknowledge me
- Take my order as soon as you are able
- Pick my food up and deliver when it is ready
- Get my bill right

I have even tipped when only one of the requests are met---acknowledge me.

The server who can find the nanosecond it takes to turn your head in my direction has done enough to earn their 20% tip.

In a weird way, I miss the times in my gourmet kitchens where precision and artistry collided on Friday and Saturday dinner nights. I was proud of the way my team performed and never forgot to thank them. As with any good team dynamic, they did some of the heavy lifting and I received all the accolades. The tradeoff was that I imparted skills and techniques which, had they chosen to pursue, would have made them highly employable and successful.

No one can ever question the "work hard, play harder" ethic my team lived by and they did it as good as anybody... I chuckle when I see a chef act like Gordon Ramsay on *Hell's Kitchen* and the things he says to his crew, berating and humiliating them.

News flash: try doing that in a real kitchen and when your guest checks start rolling off the ticker, you will be the only one to work all five stations in your kitchen. No one is going to put up with that type of shit. If a real chef has to act like that in his or her kitchen, the core reason must be that they are insecure at not being perceived as the all-knowing, all-powerful master he or she thinks they are.

Weak.

The next story deals with prejudice.

Happy Hour

I was hired to play my guitar and sing for happy hours at a local tavern only a couple miles away from the NFL stadium in Phoenix, Arizona. When I told a friend of my gig, he said "Man, I can't believe you are even allowed into that place with all the rednecks. "Prejudice," he said, "dies hard, but not in that place."

The place was a typical watering hole filled with typical working men and women (no white-collar workers here!) and the ages of the patrons varied anywhere from the minimum drinking age to some fellas that looked closer to the maximum drinking age, if there is such a thing. The jukebox was loaded with diverse music: country music, old country music, older country music, and a sprinkling of even older country music. I chuckled when I skimmed through some of the titles and in a span of about fifteen seconds or so, figured out what my playlist would look like for this motley assemblage.

I ordered a cold Bud and a shot of whiskey (just to fit in of course) and bellied up to the old wooden bar. I overheard Gary, a painter, talking to his buddy George, a plumber. I knew their names because they were wearing name patches above their shirt pockets. Gary's white overalls were splattered with many colors of different paints and George's shirt and pants, well, they had whatever plumbers spilled on them and I decided I really didn't care to know what. Both men were already half in the bag and Happy Hour was still half an hour away. Gary was telling a story about his last job painting a new addition for a client he referred to as a "bean counter" and George was laughing coarsely and loudly. *Oh brother,* I thought as I drained my shot and took a long pull on my beer. After a brief sound check of my axe and microphone, I returned to the bar where I scribbled my playlist on a couple cocktail napkins. Merle, Hank, Conway, and other giants populated the list as I surmised that even newer country and God forbid, country *rock* were out of the question tonight. After some small talk with the bartender and a trip to the outhouse (really, an outhouse!), I returned and plugged in.

I was raised with absolutely NO prejudices by my parents, and I have always considered myself accessible and tolerant of all races, colors, and creeds. Having traveled extensively overseas as a child also served to open up the world and its diverse cultures and peoples to me. My best friends in high school in England were black, but to me they were just my brothers-from-a-different-mother.

Usually, I set out a big jar for tips, and I put a little sign that designated the tips would be used for "Green Fees." I decided against that thinking *not exactly the golfing crowd here tonight.*

Earlier in the day I saw on the news that Michael Jackson, the King of Pop, had died. I grew up on his music as did many of us, and I remember taking the news particularly hard. In spite of how anyone feels about his eccentricities, there is no denying the man's genius and major impact on music in the micro and the planet in the macro. I still get chills when I recall the first time I saw him "moonwalk," his patented dance.

A strange thought occurred to me.

Think I'll shake up the County Club, I thought to myself. I decided I would begin my set with an a cappella rendition of "She's Out of My Life," one of the King's many hits.

"Hi. My name is Markus (my stage name) and I want to start out tonight with a song that I dedicate to the passing of a true music legend." As the now-full bar swiveled their squeaky bar stools in my direction, I flipped the mic switch on and gave a very soulful from-the-heart version of the classic. I was so wrapped up in the song I did not pick up on the fact the noisy room had quieted. So much so that as I belted out the last few notes, the tavern was now devoid of sound, the bartender even muting the television behind the bar. Even the pool-playing rowdies had stopped playing and turned in my direction. When I finished I opened my eyes expecting the worst. What happened next still blows my mind when I think about it.

The entire bar of typical white working men and women were actually *standing and cheering!* I received the only standing ovation I ever got in my several decades of playing music.

I can't lie, I teared up and choked out a quick "Thank you. Now let's turn the music up and the lights down. This son-of-a-bitch is now officially a honkey-tonk!"

My best solo gig ever.

As the crowd hooted and hollered approval, I turned my head to the left and caught a glimpse of the true source of prejudice in the bar.

It was my reflection in a cracked Heineken mirror looking back at me.

******

Q

Querulous implies complaining, something I do, but mostly in private. My problem is that I've never given a shit about anything, so if I don't care, I don't really have the right to complain, right? The first story has plenty of it.

A quandary, the second emotion by definition, is an uncertain state where your mind cannot or will not, make a clear-cut decision, perhaps because nothing is clear-cut anymore. In a perfect world, everyone questions everything.

In reality, very few question *anything*. As long as people are people, you (we) need to continue to ask until we are satisfied with the answer proffered. Never having to ask and never suffering injury is truly Pollyannaspeak.

Reminds me of the very first job I ever had. I was five years old when I befriended Johnny. We became best friends as we were the only American children living in the tiny Japanese village of Nakagami-Akashima. Our "compound" held four American families, and Johnny was my next-door neighbor. We both held down the same "job." We were hired by a local *papa-san* (anyone older than my brother was a *papa-san* to me) as his, for lack of a better word, slaves.

Actually, we were subcontractors, performing services for compensation. On Saturday, we would go early in the morning on his dusty wooden cart pulled by two small, but old, brown donkeys. There was a small patch of woods and Johnny, and I would fill the entire cart with wood, some pieces even too big for our little spaghetti-arms to hoist. Papa-san would sit in the cart barking orders and drinking whiskey. After what seemed like days, the cart was loaded and back we went to the village. Invariably, papa-san would have to wake us up from our exhausted sleep.

Turns out the wood was for firing the furnace for the community bathhouse, as there was no internal plumbing (outside of our compound) in the entire village. Everyone in town would eventually make their way to the bathhouse. Papa-san asked Johnny if we wanted ten-yen (about two cents) or something else. Now ten-yen might not sound like much, but it might as well have been ten million dollars to us. We could literally live for weeks off that kind of cash. Sno-cones, candies. We could get a hundred pieces of candy!

Here is where the quandary part comes in.

The "something else" papa-san offered was the opportunity to go up on the narrow, rickety bamboo walkway he had constructed his drunk-ass self. From up there you could look down on the entire bathhouse and all the naked girls, or so he claimed.

Johnny and I had a decision to make, one that could possibly be life-defining. After the torture of loading wood all day, this was really a no-brainer.

Johnny smiled at me as he flipped his ten-yen piece, dreaming of the sweet treasures to come.

He looked really small down there from the walkway.

"Holy shit! Somebody give me something *strong* to drink! Now!" he barked jokingly. A big mug of Gramma's Egg Nog was handed to him. He drained half of the potent, frothy libation in one large gulp.

"Rough night, honey?" his wife asked.

"Actually, it was a beautiful night. No emergencies or anything out of the ordinary. Just a nice quiet, snowy winter night. That is until I started for home. I saw a little brown puppy in the middle of the street, so I pulled up alongside him. He looked cold, scared, and hungry. I called out *Here little one! Here, boy!* The puppy froze and then I detected the tiniest of movement from his little tail."

"Atta boy. Where do you live,?" I asked. The little explosion of fur was now in full-blown body-wag as I eagerly
approached. I scooped the little guy up and of course the attraction was immediate and mutual."

"Sorry honey," he winked at his wife. His eyes danced as he continued. "He looked undernourished and his basic necessities were obviously not being met. I saw he did have a small rusty ID tag which was mostly obscured by fur and the wide leather collar he wore. I knew the exact address, having visited that same neighborhood before. I walked up to the front porch, trying to avoid the many piles of refuse and garbage in the yard. With the puppy cradled in my left arm, I rang the doorbell with my right. I followed the *ding-dong* with three short raps on the door."

"A little help here," he laughed, tapping the side of his empty mug for emphasis. A refill ensued with just a sprinkle of nutmeg and cinnamon.

"I raised my hand again when the door opened," he continued.

"Hello, I found this little fella here in the middle of Clayton Street, about three blocks from here. I thought I'd return him to his address listed on the tag," I said.

"Who the fuck are you? Seriously? If you stole my dog, I'll fuckin' have you killed, asshole."

I was looking into the face of pure ignorance and nothing I have ever seen before, or since, is as ugly or frightening.

"No, ma'am I am *returning* this animal."

"Well, if you think I am paying you a reward, forget it," she drawled, her eyes squinting through cigarette smoke.

"I extended the puppy and the woman tenderly accepted it. Then she threw it down violently, the animal yowling and scampering away quickly. I flinched, fighting back the urge to hit this cruel individual. It was then I saw this wasn't the only resident in need of attention. With the door wide-open I could see no fewer than fifteen dogs and at least that many cats walking around in different stages of starvation. Then the smell hit me.

"Just a sec," she said, index finger pointing skyward. She pressed her cell phone to her ear. "Yes I can hear you. Yes I can talk. Just some Christmas freak trying to extort money from me. Yes the drugs were picked up. Billy got killed. Payday, boys." She
had a sick, crooked smile on her face as her cigarette ash fell to the soiled carpet.

Two children entered the room cautiously, a four-year old boy named Max was pulling along his three-year old sister Lucy. The two were naked and dirty, their ribs and hip bones exposed through the flesh. They were dying.

I was crying inside. The children were more than filthy. I would guess they had *never* bathed in their lives.

"Hold on a sec," she barked. 'What do you two little shits want? You better get your asses to work making money or cleaning up this shithole. Those are your choices. Now get the hell out of my face. Now!"

She continued her conversation as I rose to leave.

"What exactly IS my cut? What? Oh, I can definitely live with that. The kids? What about the kids? The little losers know where to eat, shit, sleep, and watch TV. I'll leave a couple large jars of cheap peanut butter and a box of crackers on the counter. They'll be OK for a week with that. The animals? Fuck 'em. I don't feed 'em anyway. They eat what they steal at night when I let them out. I'll just leave the doors open. Don't have anything to steal anyway," she laughed, lighting up another Kool.

"I couldn't believe what I was hearing. I turned and raised my hand in farewell, not needing a mental reminder to make some phone calls when I got home."

"Merry Christmas, ma'am, I said as I turned to leave.

"Yeah, yeah fuck off", she said closing the door in my wake.

"I could not get back home to you fast enough. And here I am."

"Here you are," she smiled. They fixed their eyes on each other in a loving silence.

His wife spoke first.

"Tell you what," she started, reaching for his belt. "Gulp down that nog, have one more behind it, and I'll fill you a bowl of OG Kush. I will give you a nice Christmas foot rub, we'll listen to some jams, and you can tell me about all the *good* people you have met."

"I'm starting to believe there are NO good people. All people are shit. Evil to the core. They fuck up the planet, screw over each other, and worst of all, they poison their offspring with this same ignorance. Once the children are no longer the hope for the future, we are finished. I say fuck it all, it's over."

"You really are scaring me. Please don't think like that. As fucked up as this world is, I have to believe that *most* people, on a daily basis, will do the right thing when given two choices. Besides, what about the kids? They can't control their situations. It's not their fault. You *have* to believe that. The day that you don't, it truly *is* over."

He rose to his feet, reaching for his true love.

"Mrs. Santa Claus, I love you truly." The Christmas lights were reflecting off her round spectacle lenses.

"Mr. Santa Claus, right back at you," she laughed as she kissed him deeply.

******

Nirvana

I woke up from the soundest sleep I have ever experienced in all my sixty-five years of existence on this planet. As I stirred from my slumber, I could smell sweet honeysuckle, intoxicating jasmine, and the unmistakable perfume of roses. A light tropical breeze blew through my thick black hair and caressed my tanned, athletic body. To say I was in good shape would be the grossest of understatements. I had the body of a twenty-year-old football player. I slipped on my designer shorts and took one last glance in the full-length mirror.

My soulmate was still sleeping, the Egyptian silk sheets rising and falling with her rhythmic breathing. I watched Chopper, my German Shorthair Pointer, at the foot of our immense bed as he stirred awake. He was about to begin another day of running
and playing in the fields and valleys before splashing in the clear cool waters of the lake. I made a mental Post-it to pick him up some filet mignon for dinner.

Outside, a beautiful fawn lazed gracefully in the meadow, nuzzling its mother. Three happy little blue jays danced in concert to the strains of Led Zeppelin's *Stairway to Heaven*. The sun was bright, but not hot, as it illuminated the eastern slope of the mountain with its lush carpet of multi-colored wildflowers amid a sprinkling of Angel's Breath. The blossoms were swaying gently as several fat honeybees jockeyed for position to extract the sweet nectar. In the tree just outside the bedroom window, a nest full of baby robins chirped hungrily as a pair of bushy-tailed squirrels returned to their holes, their cheeks bulging with yummy walnuts and almonds. *Heaven*, I thought to myself.

I slipped on my sox and boxers and reached for the garment bag hanging on the bathroom door. My fifteen-thousand-dollar custom Gucci suit fit perfectly. Placing my feet into ultra-comfortable Italian leather shoes (my feet weren't sore), I spun around and returned to my dresser. Opening my jewelry box, I chose the platinum Rolex and a large gold nugget ring. After my butler tied my painted magenta silk tie, I returned to the box and selected a 10-carat pink diamond tie pin to complete the ensemble. I couldn't resist stealing another glance in the mirror. Perfect. Everything was perfect except for the rumpled newspaper laying on the floor next to the bed. I picked it up and the tear-stained pages fell open to the obituary page. I started reading: *Mark Diaz, age 65, died as a result from injuries sustained in an automobile accident…….* I looked back to the mirror for confirmation of my existence, but I showed no reflection whatsoever. However, my soulmate was looking back at me, a twisted smile on her face.

"It's true," she answered before I could open my mouth. "How many times did I plead with you about drinking and driving?"

Up until now, I was ready for a big breakfast of chicken fried steak with country white gravy, eggs, hash browns, sourdough toast, pancakes, and fresh-squeezed orange juice.

But now, feeling a sickening knot in my stomach begin to grow, I had to use the bathroom.

Fast. I frantically reached for the doorknob and twisted. *Wait, if I'm in heaven, how can the doorknob be stuck?*

"Guess again," she said, smiling as she disappeared.

******

R

Respect is and always has been, large in my life. I need to respect something before I can believe in it. Is that weird or is that just me? I respect weird things like commitment. Commitment in the form of loyalty, fearlessness, and resolve. But what about serial killers or terrorists? Are they committed? Hell yes. Do I respect them? Fuck no! But they *are* committed.

I respect someone who talks to you from the heart and not from a subliminal script learned from advertisement bombardment. You can seriously tell the difference. Even so, all it really does is highlight yet another glorious human difference.

We are truly a delicious *Gumbo humanis*.

Respect in my family was not earned, it was there for all eternity for you to pay, and rule number one if you wanted to continue living.

Let's just say you were unfortunate enough to disrespect my mother in front of the other family members at a Sunday morning breakfast. Well, before you even got a glimpse of the fresh

homemade tortillas, frijoles, chile rellenos, menudo, huevos con queso blanco, pork guisado, salsa and guacamole, you first started the respect repayment plan with a pop to the chops by the entire family. There was a definite hierarchy. Gramps first, (Gramma
never did), Aunts and Uncles next, and finally, Mom herself. A stiff price to pay and not oft-repeated.

I still say "yes ma'am and yes sir" when I address those worthy. That right there is how I was raised, pure and simple. Effective, yet all the love in the universe.

It hurts to see someone disrespected even if you don't know them. Self-disrespect is the very worst, and that hollow look in the sunken eyes of someone who has given up is a ghostly image to carry.

Reverence makes me think of religion or the Church for some reason. Reverence is respect to the nth degree and not coincidentally, the subject of the second contribution.

******

The Steam Room

Randy got to the gym at four o'clock and already the machines were filling up with weekend warriors and the serious gym rats and weight freaks, all of whom Randy envied. At least they had some purpose in their lives. They had a direction, misguided or not was not the question; they at least had a direction they were headed. Randy did too, only his direction never changed: it was always headed for trouble and the next available place to lay prone with the nicest woman he met on each day for the rest of his life. It was almost a formula.

"Hi, have a great workout! The tight little attendant cheered as she swiped the Member ID badge.

Pretty.

Young.

Pink hair.

Black fingernail polish.

When am I going to stop looking at every single woman on the planet and not think of sleeping with them? What age? Randy got no answer from himself and headed to the locker room.

It was not the same locker room he had been hanging his clothes in and taking his showers in for the past three years. There were large blocks of concrete and tile dug up all through what was once the men's locker room. The sinks and urinals had been removed, leaving a stained sheet of once-white porcelain to lend its unique fragrance to the room. Holes in the floor and wall marked where the sink pipes had been removed. Over the exposed plaster ceiling was a hand-painted sign with an arrow that said "Steam." He grabbed a towel and headed down the narrow passageway.

Randy glimpsed through the glass and saw that the steam had just started a new cycle. He liked it because this gym had nice long fifteen-minute cycles in the steam room. The steam room got really hot and stayed that way for a long time, so it was not for the faint of heart. Randy figured any day now some old fart would complain, and they'd overcompensate and go back to the five-minute cycles.

Randy hung up his towel on the stainless-steel hook and slipped through the door like a ninja. It is common steam room etiquette to enter and leave a "live" steam room so as to allow as little as possible of the fat-melting steam to escape. Randy climbed up to the third row of tiled seating and strained to make out the other figures in the room. As the room filled with steam, it became impossible to see six inches through the dense fog. After the entire room completely filled with hot steam, the shut-off valve kicked in and the room went silent.

He heard four others enter the room and find seats. He could hear snippets of their exchanges, something like aviators might discuss lift, cruising altitude, ordinance. Ordinance.

Definitely military.

"Excuse me, I can't see you, but I overheard you talking. Are you pilots?" Randy broke the silence with his query.

"Gentlemen! Sound off! The command came from the voice in the corner of the room.

"Briggs, Jack, Naval Aviator, sir!" A rather deep voice boomed.

"Natson, Richard, Naval Aviator, sir!"

"Bryce, Shannon, Flight Surgeon, sir!" The doctor spoke in a much higher voice, almost tinny.

"And I am Sam Kelly, Commanding Officer," the deepest voice from the corner boomed. "This is my flight crew. At ease gentlemen" Sam barked. The other three pilots chuckled at the impromptu roll call.

"And you sir?"

"My name is Randy Ball. I didn't mean to impose; I've always been interested in flight and flying. Are you stationed at Pensacola?"

"Negative. We are here on TDY from Nellis Air Force Base in Las Vegas. We are participating in some "war games" training on the new F-35 Lightning II.

We're only here for a month."

The steam was still dense preventing any line of sight. Randy knew TDY was an acronym for temporary duty but didn't know a Lightning II from Adam.

Jack Briggs was first to rise and stepped right by Randy. He could see Jack was a stout, well-muscled guy with a short military haircut. He was naked as a jaybird and no matter how hard he strained to see, Randy could not see one pound of extra flesh on his frame.

"See you on the B-Ball court," he said to his mates as he slipped out the door.

"Did you see the body on that new nurse? What's her name Doc? Oh yeah, Maggie. Smokin' hot!" Rick Natson was all riled up, speaking loudly now.

Dr. Cannon replied "Yes, she is quite an attractive young lady."

Randy held the theory that if he were not in the room the flight crew would be using much more descriptive and colorful adjectives to describe this nurse.

Dr. Cannon rose and walked around a puddle on the floor, taking him within a foot of Randy's face. He winked and leaned in for clarification, "she is the hottest piece of ass we have ever seen in the hospital, sir."

So much for Randy's theory.

Randy could not get over how young this doctor looked. Of course, at sixty-five, he could not believe how young *everybody* looked.

He sat back, a little more comfortable now. He saw an opportunity to join the convo.

"So, you say this nurse is smokin' hot?" He turned toward the general vicinity of Rick Natson's voice.

"Sir, would you care to elaborate?" Rick looked to his commanding officer.

Sam thought about it and then replied.

"Affirmative on Aviator Natson's observations. This girl is about six foot tall, a fine body including an ass you could crack walnuts with. She has a rack that I could well, let's just say I would welcome the chance to make her curl up her toes and scream my name in the dark. I certainly would NOT kick her out of the sack!"

"Smokin' hot," Rick said as he rose to leave.

"Sounds awesome Sam. Is it ok if I call you Sam?"

Sam Kelly stood, extending a hand to shake. "Sam or Samantha.
Either or."

As Naval Aviator Commanding Officer Samantha Kelly slid out the door, the steam had cleared just enough for Randy to make out her near-perfect body.

Holy shit.

******

Rice and Fish

Maruku-san spoke in a most reverent tone of the artifacts he stumbled upon while strolling through an overgrown field. It was a warm Sunday afternoon, and he had no real desire to sort through the remains of an honored elder's life, but here they were, in a small pile at his feet.

The carved wooden rice bowl was still functional; it had escaped the ignominious fate of its successors, the ornately-
painted ceramic vessels. The masculine chopsticks, chipped and splintered, lay neatly to the side in preparation for yet another modest portion of rice and fish.

The foggy yellow lenses of the frail, wire-rimmed spectacles were not as fortunate. They had witnessed eighty-seven years of rich life on Honshu Island and were no longer needed.

Kneeling, without a sound, he picked up a tiny wooden box and carefully opened it. Inside there were three tarnished gold teeth. The sight of them brought a smile to Maruku-san's face.

Replacing everything in the most exact manner possible, he turned to leave. He could not make out the name on the small, crumbling headstone, but he hoped they liked the rice and fish.

******

S

Sadistic is my first choice for this letter. Several of my works qualify under this heading, but *Attention to Detail* is the story that gave me the most creeps while I was typing it out. All the creepier because *it could actually happen.* I hope to God it never happens again.

The second tale is the longest in the book. It chronicles a group of kids growing up in Anywhere, USA. I remember when I would leave the house after eating an early breakfast and be gone for the entire day. Doing what? Playing! That thing where you are NOT on a cell phone, or tablet, or computer, and where imagination was NOT just another download in your folder.

Make believe.

Exercise.

Fun.

Sound familiar?

One of the worst things about technology is that people, specifically kids, rely too much on electronics to communicate. While there is most certainly a time and place, the last time I checked, this world was still managed by people. Talking. The
lost art of conversation. The Gift of Gab is one of the most precious gifts of all, increasing in value by the minute.

I love surprises. Surprise parties are the best, especially when the surprisee hates surprises. Scary surprises are the very best. I will laugh for hours on end watching those videos where people *really* scare the shit out of some poor unsuspecting person. I know, not PC, but still funny as hell.

I used to hide around hallway corners in our house waiting for my stepfather to arrive. I would leap out, scream "boo!" at the top of my lungs and literally bring myself to tears watching him turn crimson and get *so* pissed. I thought it was the funniest thing ever. I did it at least three times a week. Eventually, I would begin chuckling in anticipation of my scary leap and Vern would hear me and sneak up on *me* and yell. He completely turned the tables on me. I don't think I did it much after that.

It wasn't nearly as funny.

******

Attention to Detail……Sadistic

They finally did it. We asked them to stop, but they had to
keep fucking with us. The world needs less evil…….

0458 hrs: Steven and Robbie woke up simultaneously, one on top of the other, two minutes before the alarm buzzer intruded. Robbie reached over and ended the threat.

0515 hrs: Robbie performs his wifely duties in the shower for Steven in preparation for the Big Day.

0535 hrs: Robbie makes breakfast. Not a word is spoken.

Breakfast consumed.

0620 hrs: Weapons check:

- Two Mauser short-stock sniper rifles. Built for mobility and extremely powerful with laser scope. Three hundred rounds of ammunition.
Check.
- Remington sawed-off .12-gauge shotgun. Scatter-shot and low gauge to ensure maximum collateral damage. Two boxes shells.
Check.
- Two modified M-14 sniper rifles. One hundred shells. Deadly accurate *and perfect for picking off assholes* Steven thought to himself. Check.
- Eight chemical grenades. Check.
- Eight fragmentation grenades designed for 360-degree shrapnel radius. Check.
- Two Smith & Wesson .38 caliber pistols. One cox of .38 caliber hollow-point bullets. Check.

Everything was packed into two military issued combat duffels, large enough to carry a .50 Cal and twenty clips. Robbie winked at Steven.

0700 hrs: The boys load up their car, a 1956 Hearse they bought two weeks ago with the last of their school trust funds.

0721 hrs: Hearse pulls onto school service road after Stephen uses bolt cutters to snap the lock.

0725 hrs: Circular glass cutting tool allows access through Science Lab window. Robbie drops the duffel bags onto the floor, climbs through and reaches for Stephen's outstretched hand.
"Thanks honey", Stephen coos.

0730 hrs: First school bus arrives. Robbie rose and handed Stephen his duffel. Like clockwork, practiced time and again, the boys tucked the .38's in their belts in unison.

"It's time," Stephen says, straightening Robbie's collar and adjusting his fragmentation grenade belt.

0733 hrs.   The cafeteria is filled to capacity for the breakfast hour. 250 students.

0734 hrs: As scripted and planned out a hundred times, the boys burst through the doors screaming "This is for YOU fuckheads!"

0735 hrs: Death toll 201

0755 hrs: As all hell breaks loose, Stephen turns to Robbie, mouthing the words "I love you." The boys raise the pistols to their temples and pull their triggers one last time.

******

The Freak

"Hey freak!" Ronnie yelled.

"Hey freak-o!" his friend Stevie chimed in.

"Look over here, you weird A-hole!"

The pack of boys scattered in search of projectiles to launch at Danny Frako.

Danny Freak-o, he muttered under his breath as he pushed open the tattered screen door to Sam's Store.

"We'll get you freak-o!"

"You're dead meat!"

"Get out and stay out!"

Danny jumped on his off-road bike and looked back, flipping off the boys as they swore ungodly revenge. *The fuck they know?* Danny asked no one and tore away on his green ten-speed, leaving a rooster tail of dusty pebbles and dirt.

By noon, the youths assembled on John's front lawn. John entered the center of the circle and the others fanned out to give him more room. John started drawing lines in the dirt with his finger.

"Ronnie, you and Stevie gather as many rocks as you can find and stockpile them here and here…." He pointed with his dirty finger.

Little Stevie Crown jumped to his feet. "Aye aye, sir!" Stevie was the only kid in the neighborhood who spoke Navy, the others preferring the less-romantic "Yessir" or "Yes General sir." Stevie's big brother Patrick had enlisted in the "real" military and was stationed in the Philippines.

Ronnie glared at Stevie. *Stevie is only ten and he is only a private,* Ronnie thought. *I'm the sergeant! I should answer first!*

"Yes General!" Ronnie straightened to attention.

He and Stevie were the only two enlisted men in the neighborhood "army." The other boys were officers of various ranks and titles: captains, lieutenants, majors, corporals, colonels, and even a self-appointed ten-star General----John. Ronnie definitely knew the pecking order, especially near the bottom of the totem pole, where he and Stevie remained. If nothing else, he was still above the lowest rung on the totem pole---Stevie.

John continued drawing in the dirt between clumps of sandy, limp crabgrass, issuing missions, raids, and ensuring his orders were clearly understood. All orders involved one crystalline, unified objective: the death of the enemy (Danny).

John stood up and continued. "O.K. everyone has a mission in this war…."

"Sir? Uh General sir?" A shaky voice attached to the small body of Kenny Sillson took center stage.

"Major?" John bellowed, raising his left eyebrow.

"Uh General Sir, why do we have to kill Dan…, er, uh I mean the enemy? The little boy's eyes were wide, awash with fear and curiosity.

"You mean why do we want to kill D-A-N-N-Y? There I spelled it out for everyone. Who wants to start?" John's steely grey eyes challenged his charges. John looked to Freddy Mitchell. "Freddy?"

"That asshole stole my bicycle! I told his parents, the cops, even the principal, and no one did anything about it. I know he did it. I saw him." He laughed in my face and said if I ever get another one, he will steal it too." Freddy looked down. "My parents don't have the money to get me another bike."

A line of eager witnesses formed behind Freddy, each with a story about the evil Danny and how he had wronged them and theirs.

"D-d-d-d Danny took my lunch m-m-money, Barry stuttered. Lots of t-t-t-times." Barry sat and Buddy stood.

"Danny hurt my little sister. The police got him," Buddy began.

The rambunctious army quieted down, recognizing the seriousness of this testimony. The boys strained to hear every word.

"He pushed his way through the back door when I was closing it. Mom and Dad were bowling that night. Danny hit me hard…." Buddy rotated slowly, lifting his Raiders jersey for all to see his badge of honor. Buddy fought back tears. "He hurt my little sister Rosie. He had her locked in the bathroom with him. She was crying and *screaming*. I called the bowling alley and Mom had me call 9-1-1. I never found out what happened, but Danny was back at school the next day! It's just not fair"….Buddy's words trailed off. He looked back to John.

"How about you General sir?" Buddy asked. "Why do YOU want him killed?"

"Never mind!" John snapped. His troops looked around nervously. John, sensing revolt, more evenly now, continued. "I have my own reason, and the more I hear from you all…" Well, I just *know* that prick deserves everything we give him!"

"Well, is that it? Anyone else with a good reason to kill the enemy?" John was daring his troops now.

John was exhorting his army now, whipping them into a frenzy.

"Kill! Kill! Kill! Kill!" The war chant grew in intensity.

"Who wants Kool-Aid? Cookies?" Mom was holding a frosty pitcher of blue delight.

Gotta love Moms and their impeccable sense of timing.

The rations consumed; the boys gathered around John.

"Uh, General Sir" Kenny Sillson stood again.

"Major?"

"The enemy, Danny", he strained. "Has to die because"….Kenny looked around cautiously now. "Danny has to die because he killed my little kitten Jinks and…." His small voice trailed off. John was growing impatient with Major Sillson.

"Major, is that *all*? Spill it!" John leaned in.

"Because I saw him with Buttons on the day he went missing. I think he killed your puppy!" Kenny screamed.

"Gotta go now," John said as he took the steps three at a time and sprinted inside, slamming the front door behind him.

John sat on his bed and eased back, his head resting on the flat white pillow. He looked to his dresser and the picture of his dearly departed furry

friend Buttons. He was only four months old when he went "missing." He always suspected Danny Freak-o of taking Buttons, but he never had any proof; only the well-deserved suspicion Frako enjoyed in the neighborhood. He had stopped them in the little community park where John had taken his pup for his very first walk. John loved watching the clumsy little fellow as he sniffed everything in sight, sending his tail whipping every which way. He was a Dachshund, short and brown with a black birthmark on his pointy nose. It was shaped like a button and made it easy for John to name him. John had begged for years, it seemed, to get a puppy. His parents finally relented on John's last birthday, and he was only two weeks away from his tenth. John sat upright and swung his legs over the side
of the bed. He picked up the second picture sitting on his dresser, this one of his little Calico kitten.

"Buttons I'll get him. I promise," he vowed.

John decided it was time to find out *for certain* that the Freak had caused his grief. He didn't have to wait long.

It was another hot summer day, and John decided to head to the quarry for a swim. As he approached the chalky-white limestone formation, he saw a green ten-speed parked at the entrance to the quarry.

His bike.

John footed his kickstand and parked his bike. He immediately thought of Freddy Mitchell and the bike he lost to the Freak. He started walking to the steps leading below to the diving platform when three junior high punks approached, forming a barrier, their arms on their hips.

"Hey shithead, what are you doing coming to our swimming hole?" Bill Ganz was an eighth-grader and the biggest thug in the school. John was glad the bully would be long gone by the time he hit junior high.

"Look," John pleaded. "I don't want any trouble. I'll just leave." John was genuinely getting scared now as the boys circled him.

"Grab the little son-of-a-bitch," Bill ordered his two accomplices. The two obliged, each grabbing one of John's sweaty arms. The pair walked their victim to Bill.

"You and your little faggot "army" are no longer welcome here," Bill began, pointing in John's face. "Go the fuck home and here's something to remember us by." He punched John in the
nose, sending a shock through his head and blood spewed everywhere.

"Please," John sputtered. "I'll just leave. Please. Leave me alone."

"Fuck him up!" Bill ordered.

John braced for a real beating.

The two boys each hit him in the stomach and John fell to the ground crying.

At that instant, Danny Frako climbed the last of the steps and spied the situation. Without saying a word, he tackled Bill. Surprised, Bill called for his two henchmen to assist. John was lying motionless, afraid any activity would bring a continuance of the thrashing. Danny was no match for Bill, and when the other two joined in, it was all over but the bleeding. They took turns punching and kicking Danny for about three minutes. Bill remained still, feigning unconsciousness. The three boys were laughing now, as they grabbed their towels and headed down the steps. Danny lay motionless, but he was not acting.

John, fearing the boys would return, got up and rode away on his bike, leaving Danny broken and bleeding.

The next day, word had spread about the beatings at the quarry. John's nose was bandaged with two little breathing holes which allowed painful breaths for his smashed nose. Evidently, Danny was taken to the hospital with broken ribs and a concussion. John still couldn't believe how his hated and feared enemy had come to his aid without as much as a second's hesitation.

After three days, the pounding in John's head subsided and he made a big decision. He had to find out from Danny himself the reason he took a beating for a guy who was obviously an enemy.

"Man, I saw those three assholes beating you up and that is just not right," Danny wheezed. His torso was wrapped around with bandages as the nurse checked his chart and adjusted the oxygen being pumped into Danny's nose through a little plastic tube.

"Yeah, but Danny, look at what happened to you. I wanted to thank you for that. I know we aren't exactly friends, but thank you anyway," John thought this the ultimate irony. Here he was *thanking* the Freak.

"It's just not right," Danny mumbled as the nurse inserted a needle with morphine into his bruised right arm. John got up and left the hospital room.

It was a full month before John and his "army" reunited on John's front lawn.

"We heard you and the Freak were in a fight at the quarry", Kenny Sillson stated. The others in the group nodded in unison. "Are we gonna get him now?"

"Not just yet. I'm still planning," John fibbed.

Danny Frako was sent home after a full five weeks in the hospital. The first visitor to come knocking was none other than John.

"Hey."

"Hey," Danny mumbled back.

"You okay?" John approached Danny as he sat propped up on the couch.

"Still sore, but I'll be okay. Hey John, thanks for coming to see me. Nobody else probably will."

Just at that exact moment, a tiny black fur ball bounded into the room, his little round belly barely clearing the couch as he started licking furiously at his best friend Danny.

"Chico, my little friend," Danny said with obvious love in his voice.

"Is he yours?" John couldn't believe his eyes. Danny, the Freak, actually loved animals! How could he possibly hurt Buttons, or any other animal? John was still having trouble figuring out why the Freak had taken such an ass-whipping for him.

"Yeah, that's my little boy," Danny wheezed through his bandages. "You can pet him; he's really friendly. He loves it if you scratch him behind his head, on the top of his neck."

John scratched as instructed and the cat began purring loud enough that both boys started laughing in tandem.

"Gotta go. We're having Sloppy Joes tonight for supper, John said as he rose.

"You really know how to hurt a guy," Danny joked, wincing, and clutching his ribcage.

Two months later, John was just finishing mowing the lawn and was sitting on his porch steps when, who should approach but Danny Frako.

"Hi John," he said.

"Hey what's up?"

"Have you got a minute? It's really important. I have to show you something." Danny was imploring.

""Can I take a shower first?" John asked.

"No. Please. Come now." John started down the street and he continued talking. "I had a lot of time to think while I was laid up at home and the things I hear others say I am responsible for, well I have to show you." They stopped in front of a grey and white Cape Cod draped by maple giants.

Danny turned left into the driveway and slipped into the unlocked back gate of the wooden fence.

John stopped short of going in. "Danny what the hell?"....

Danny emerged with a bicycle. Not any bicycle, Freddy Mitchell's bicycle.

"No one believed me when I said I didn't do it," Danny explained.

John could not help himself. He had to ask.

"Danny, that thing with Buddy's little sister. I mean.."

"John, come on. I was teasing her by holding onto her doll and the next thing the cops come. Do you think I could go back to school the very next day if I did something? Man, I thought we were becoming friends. Guess I was wrong. Sorry…."

"Danny wait. Can you meet me in front of my house on the lawn today at 2? I wanna set some things straight with the gang."

"I'll be there," Danny smiled.

Everyone was represented at the summit that ten-star General John had called for. There were a lot of quizzical faces directed at John and the presence seated behind him.

The Freak.

"Okay everyone. I'll make this short. During the last several months, I have come to know Danny Frako and I now know that he has been wrongly accused and misunderstood and…"

Kenny, Stevie, Ronnie, Buddy, and even little Freddy Mitchell all shouted in protest.

"Freddy!" John barked, as if from nowhere Danny appeared with Freddy's bike.

"What the?" Freddy stammered taking the handlebars from Danny.

"Freddy, gang", he said facing the army. "I know for a fact Danny did not take the bike and in fact, he is the one who found the bike.

Freddy looked dazed.

"As leader of this army I say we let Danny into the gang, and we all start over as friends. Now let Danny speak in his own behalf."

"It's all yours," he said as he turned to Danny. Danny stooped to John's ear and whispered.

"Thanks John-boy. Very smooth. Like that nasty little sister of Buddy's. And like the snap you hear when you crack a pretzel. That was the sound your little dog Buttons' neck made when I killed him."

******
T

I had to include a story about tranquility amidst all my other zaniness. No prettier a setting than the Hawaiian Islands.

Trust, the second emotion, is *huge*. I am way too trusting a person. I believe because of my insular childhood I felt no reason to distrust anyone. Unfortunately, that does not prove costly until *after* the trusted person does something untrustworthy. In spite of the injury I have suffered through mistrust, I hope I never become a frightened, bitter, hateful person. I have encountered several in my lifetime and they all wear the same face of loneliness. For some unknown reason, when someone (anyone!) says "trust me," my knee-jerk reaction is to NOT trust them.

I actually trust very few people. If I trust someone, I will think nothing at all of lending (or giving) them what they needed with a mere ask. I am far too proud to ask, but I think if someone sacrifices his or her dignity to resort to begging for

119

help, I will make the effort to give of myself to them, usually in the form of food and water. I especially don't trust myself. I am far too egomaniacal, proud, and emotional. This combination does not always allow for rational, impartial decisions. Trust is earned, not confirmed with a meaningless order. I am sure those same words were at one time spoken by all the greats, including Madoff and Ponzi.

The ability to ruin lives is a caustic reminder that money may not be the root of *all* evil, but it has to be a very close second. The things people will do for money makes me shudder to think about. Distrustful people make me sick. They are only one small step lower than an actual criminal; they just haven't been caught yet. If you see one, look away. They are to be derided and *othered* to the point of extinction.

I won't name names, but the people I do not trust all have one common denominator.

They are like me.

＊＊＊＊＊＊

Flight of Fancy……Tranquil

Kit was on top of the world. Literally. He looked out over the many shades of pink, blue, grey, and purple swirls as he headed for Hawaii. The sun was a curious orange as it slowly shed its warmth and poked its head over the horizon. Over the din of the engine, he started humming a tune his dear mother used to sing to him when he was a child. He remembered how sweet and soft her voice was, soothing any and all troubles a three-year old boy could generate. She always smelled like the small pink and white blossoms she cared for all around their modest three-room house. Although she had made her own heaven on earth and had departed seven years ago, he still missed her terribly. He wiped the tears from his eyes and blinking rapidly, set his gaze on the picture he had taped just over the altimeter gauge on the control panel.

"Suzy? Jonny?" he called out loud. "I hope you can both hear me wherever you are this morning. I really wish I could be there to take you to church and then go to the beach for a nice picnic. I miss you so much."

Kit reached for the picture and held it up in the expanding sunlight. He had been away from home now for almost six months
and the tears returned, rolling down his cheeks and forming a small puddle on his thigh. At least he was able to speak to his beloved children yesterday. Jonny was so excited about the toy airplane Kit had bought him for his birthday. It was just like the one his Dad was flying, and Jonny swore he would someday fly a real plane. Just like Dad.

"When are you coming home Daddy?" his little boy had asked.

"What, are you kidding? I'm there with you right now," Kit had assured his son. "Do you feel something tingly around your shoulder? That's me."

"I feel it Daddy!" Suzy had shouted. "I feel you here on my shoulder."

Kit's father grabbed the phone from Suzy and offered the words Kit was waiting for. "The kids are fine, son. We're all anxiously awaiting your return."

He thought of his lovely soulmate Aneka. She left this planet to begin the next sphere of existence on the very day she gave birth to her second child Jonny. She cried with joy when the nurse held her son up in front of her. She knew how much it meant to Kit, and she really believed she now had the perfect family.

Aneka died in her sleep that night.

A gust of wind snapped Kit back into the here and now as he approached the coast of the Jewel of the Pacific. Hawaii. He wondered how many islands laid claim to that nickname. Hundreds, he guessed. But this truly had to be *the* jewel. The sloping green mountains ending at water's edge. The fantastic, intoxicating tropical flowers and plants carpeting the fiftieth state. People dancing to ukulele music, laughing, and playing all along the coastline. He smiled broadly as he thought of Aneka. He pictured himself and his perfect family frolicking and making sandcastles, venturing out into the clear water to cool off. He thought of making a fire to roast hot dogs and marshmallows after the sun had retired for the evening. Aneka's premature departure had left Kit with a hole in his heart that would never close.

Now approaching eight o'clock on this beautiful December morning, Kit kissed his children's picture, stuffed it in his jacket pocket and turned south, angling downward at top speed. The engine whined and screamed as it was pushed to its absolute limit.

Six seconds later, Kit was part of a gas and oil fireball on the deck of the USS West Virginia which would soon be at the bottom of the beautiful blue waters of Pearl Harbor.

******

Closing Time

At approximately 1:30 am Eastern Standard Time, at a family-dining chain restaurant in central Florida, an ex-employee pushed his way through the back door and into the kitchen. His two friends quickly darted past, much to the surprise of the hapless dishwasher.

The kitchen was immaculate, as he knew it would be. The Associate Manager was in the office accounting for the daily sales, just as he knew he would be. There were no waiters, just the night maintenance guy, the manager, and Flo, the closing waitress.

This was going to be *easy*.

Imran walked out to the front of the restaurant as his two associates checked out the dining room and the restrooms.

Florence Summers was twenty-two years old, drop-dead gorgeous, and graduating from the University of Florida with a pre-med springboard to Johns Hopkins Medical School where she had already been accepted. She really hated the closing shift. She finished counting, picked up her guest checks, rolled her bills into a wad, and placed it in her purse. *Almost enough for my first car* she thought.

Imran ambled around the corner, startling her.

"Imran! What?"...She was looking at the automatic pistol in his left hand.

"Take it easy Flo, everything's gonna be OK. No one is going to get hurt," Imran offered. He really liked Flo and thought they would make a good couple. She was always so nice to him and always took time to sit down and speak with him in the break room when she was able. She was nice to everybody, one of the genuinely good people who worked here and treated him with *respect.*

Imran, what are you doing? Are you robbing us? Do you want my tip money?" She was extending her wad of fifty dollars to him like a child.

Imran was embarrassed by this gesture of terror and the look on Flo's face.

"No. No, Flo. Put your money away. I would never hurt you or take anything from you. Please." He gestured to her to put her money back.

"Come with me. We are going to take the money from the office and go. You don't need to fear anything. Just go along with us. We're going to put you in the walk-in and leave. I will call the police when we leave to come and get you out of the reefer. Come. You shall see."

Imran guided her to the kitchen where Franco and Noki were waiting nonchalantly, their guns listlessly dangling by their sides.

They smiled as Imran approached.

"How long?" Imran asked.

"Two minutes," Noki shot back while rolling up his sleeve to read his watch dial.

"Come on Flo. Just wait in here. I'll be right back," Imran assured her.

"I know you know this isn't right Imran, but I also know you feel like this is what you have to do to survive, so I wish you good luck in your future," Flo said as she entered the walk-in cooler.

Brandon, the fifty-year-old maintenance man was shivering in the rear of the cooler, waving his arms to keep warm. He looked scared. They both turned to the door as Noki locked it from the outside.

"Brandon, it's OK. I talked with Imran and he assured me they were only going to take the money. We are going to be fine," she assured Brandon.

"Seriously? I know it's corny, but I am too young to die," Brandon chattered nervously.

"No, don't worry. I trust Imran. He's a nice young man; he is just really confused right now. I hope he doesn't get hurt in his recklessness is all," Flo said as she rubbed her arms.

At that moment, the cooler fan stopped spinning, instantly bringing a sense of warmth and hope to the two hostages.

As the manager emerged from the office, the thieves shoved their stolen guns in his face and had him empty the safe of its contents.

Now laughing and joking, they assured the manager all they wanted was the money and that nobody would be harmed.

"Everyone just stay calm and remain here until the police arrive, which will be in a few minutes. I turned the cooler off, so you won't be too uncomfortable," Imran said as he looked into Flo's brightening face.

The entire time, Rick Speers, the Associate Manager, was staring at Imran. He wanted to be able to give a crystal-clear account as a main witness to this crime. He entered the cooler joining Flo and Brandon.

Imran stepped back and out of the cooler. He motioned to Noki and Franco.

They removed the lock, opened the cooler door, and opened fire, killing all three people.

******

U

Personally, the most annoying of all things is nagging. Since <u>my</u> wife would <u>never</u> engage in such activity, this is the imaginary scenario: she says something which is totally false, established as fact and universally accepted by all on the planet but HER. I, er, I mean this imaginary person, can show her online, in print, video, TV, it doesn't matter. She will still insist she is right! It's like her insistence on using Google to direct her movements. Drives me absolutely nuts. Imagine you are driving on a country road, and your destination is the heart of downtown. But she doesn't care.

You might say something completely innocent like "Gee, honey, it looks like we are going away from downtown."

"No. Google said fifteen miles and we've gone only fourteen."

That's when this imaginary friend of mine strangles her.

Unrelenting.

Like a puppy's curiosity. Like a newborn baby's crying and pooping. Like a mother and father's love for their children. Unrelenting like a bettor's thirst for action. Like my love for Notre Dame football. Like an alcoholic's taste for the grape. Like life and unfortunately, death.

Like a New York woman.

Now before I'm accused of bashing, let me state that I absolutely *adore* New York women. Their straightforward, no-bullshit-get-the-job-done (or I got nothing for 'ya) attitude I consider sexy as hell. I am sure I could never be actually *married* to one, as I like the attitude on occasion as opposed to unrelenting.

I once had a New York girl tell me, "you're the kind of boy no girl *wants* to meet, but every girl *has* to meet, at least once in their lifetime." After 45 years, I still don't know if that was a compliment or a shot. I guess that's another thing I like about New York women.

I can't mention New York without saying something about the Yankees. The Evil Empire. I never got that. Reviled by opponents because they <u>win</u> so much.

ANY organization that has enjoyed that much success over the years is to be lauded and emulated. I am also NOT a Yankees fan (I bleed Dodger Blue), but you have to respect them either way.

******

Move Away

God, you are beautiful. As usual. On my way here, I was thinking about our first date. How you made me laugh. I felt so comfortable. We must have laughed for hours. Who'd have thought that fifteen years later you'd still be laughing—or at least pretending to laugh—at my corny old jokes? Of course, I remember the dress. I BOUGHT it for you in Cabo San Lucas last year. Now THAT was a day to remember. The thing I remember most about that day was getting caught in that afternoon shower with you. I recall pulling you close and kissing your sweet soft lips. The water was perfect. Deep. Turquoise blue like your eyes. I remember the pact we made that day to move away to Cabo…To move away…Move away…

"Please move away from the casket, son. Let the others see
her too."

******

V

I don't know if it is a sin, but it shouldn't be. I mean where does taking pride in your appearance to an extreme become injurious? I think it is where the vain person believes their appearance somehow makes them better than anyone else. That falls more into the category of foible or fault.

No one is better than anyone else. Everyone has something inside them that is beautiful just awaiting its chance to surface.

The truly blessed emerge early and develop over time to the benefit of all. This is how the planet improves.

The biggest insult you could direct at me would be to call me arrogant or entitled. I envy no one and I root for everyone. For those who have way more than they need, I root for them to keep their wealth and share if able with those less fortunate. It is absolutely no one's obligation to share or help others, and when someone goes above and beyond with their generosity, I smile knowing it is not only a nice thing to do, but the right thing to do. And the Good Lord hard-wired me to where I believe I would maintain the same mindset if I were one of the haves. At least I really hope so.

Vanity is also a temporary condition. How can one maintain vanity as the ravages of time take their toll on the mind and body? All you have to do is look at some of the posted pictures online of aging movie stars and models to see that their vanity indeed had a start *and* end date.

Anything after the end date just indicates a dying attempt to clutch at the fleeting memory of youth and beauty. That is another reason we all need to look deeper than the face and body when evaluating a person. I think there is so much you can gain by gazing into the eyes of someone.

Pain, joy, optimism, and other emotions can be gauged by looking past the Maybelline and Revlon. Go deep. Past the manscara (I just made up another word) and guy-liner.

To the soul……

******

Dr. Richard……Vanity

Dr. Richard entered the room as if expecting applause *and he did it every time.*

"OK, let's see what we have today," he barked clinically as he carefully studied his patient. He started his head-to-toe examination by announcing to the only other person in the room, Nurse Madison, "Let's proceed….

Under the surgical mask Nurse Madison rolled her eyes at the egomaniacal Doctor Richard.

Oh brother, she thought.

"He's lying flat as a drawing," the doctor observed. "The patient is a white male, approximately forty years old," he began. Black hair, slightly obese."

"There are signs of numerous surgeries starting with the mid-cranium, it looks like the patient suffered several diseases over the course of his life."

She was staring at him now, having no earthly idea what he was talking about. She knew it had something to do with the head.

"Sponge!" the doctor barked.

The nurse bristled at the command. She reluctantly patted the smooth forehead of Dr. Richard. *Not even a thank you.* She remained silent and cool to the grossly inept surgeon. *If he even <u>was</u> a doctor.*

"There is thyroid cartilage deposit mid-larynx, nothing unusual here. OK. Shoulders both intact, in high left-chest area, the *furcula* is prominent yet normal, the patient had had open-heart surgery, the viscus of the cardiac muscle…Sponge!"

"Mom! Tell Ricky to stop yelling at me!" Madison cried.

"Will you two put away that fucking
Operation game and
wash for supper?

"Now!"

******

W

Two rules about worrying:
1--Don't sweat the small stuff.
2--It's all small stuff.

Change what you are able, but don't beat yourself up if you can't facilitate the change you desire. Always move positively in the direction you choose to take and change will occur, just possibly not at the rate you desire.

Patience.

Energy expended on worrying can best be used constructively to ensure your anticipated fears are not realized in the first place. Some people, for whatever reason, have to worry about something to maintain their personal constitution. It is merely another reminder of the glorious differences of the human race, the only race with no finish line or finishers.

It is easy for me to sit here and type don't worry, but the truth is *everyone* worries about something. Even those who will tell you they have absolutely no worries. I don't waste much time at all worrying, but when I do, it is usually related to the family and more specifically, my wife. My greater worries are more concerns than worry. I am concerned that there will be a clean, non-injurious planet that we can continue to cling to as it hurtles through space. I am concerned that we have still yet to learn from past mistakes of the wasteful folly of war and acrimony on a global scale. I am concerned that there will be enough potable water to meet the increasing needs of our voracious appetite. I am concerned that fast-food companies will continue to poison and promote obesity in our children by targeting their overwrought working mothers with lucratively low prices and availability. I am concerned that our nation continues to fall behind other nations who place the proper emphasis in providing accessible education to their citizens. I am concerned that my nieces will be able to succeed at whatever they choose to do. I am concerned with the health of my relatives, and I am concerned that I will go to the big football stadium in the sky without seeing my beloved Fighting Irish win another National Championship.

But I don't worry about it.

Waste of time.

******

More Than Concern

It was unbearably cold and the freezing rain was blowing at sharp angles as Kevin Massa tightened his grip on the steering wheel. The usually calming drive home had turned into a perilous muddy slide up the serpentine road home.

Thank God for four-wheel drive he thought.

He had called the house and then her cell phone, but Barb wasn't picking up for some unknown reason and Kevin was worried. He left work early, something he had not done in the past several years at the sporting goods store. He continued on his way, sliding, and skidding through the mud. He swiped at his glasses, fogging up as the cold lenses were assaulted with a wave of warmth from the overworked heater. Rounding the final curve, he pulled to an abrupt stop and took the front porch steps two at a time, twisting the doorknob open.

His brother John appeared in the doorway, blotting out all light from the porch light with his massive frame.

"What the hell bro?" he asked. "Why the frantic call?"

Kevin had picked up his daughter Kacey, at nineteen months, just able to say two- and three-word sentences. She pointed at everything as her young mind developed.

"Mama Baby," she said and began to cry. She raised her chubby little index finger and pointed to the front door.

Almost on cue, the doorbell rang.

"Kevin, is everything alright? My Dad could barely get me up here. He told me to call when I am ready to be picked up. Wait, where's Barb?"

Linda had only been hired two weeks ago as babysitter.

"Linda, you watch Kacey. John let's go," Kevin said without answering. He gently handed his daughter to Linda. He grabbed two flashlights from the closet and tossed one to John.

The two men darted down the front porch and into the night. Moving willfully to avoid slipping and falling in the mud, both had their flashlights focused on the ground about ten feet in front of them. They trudged on in silence, their eyes scouring every inch of Kevin's acre-sized front yard.

"I'm really worried, man," Kevin said first. "Barb would never leave Kacey. Never."

John couldn't tell whether his brother was crying or just wiping the freezing sleet from his eyes. "Kev, we'll find her. Keep moving."

"Hey, what's that? John had stopped moving his flashlight.

Kevin was kneeling, reaching down to the prone figure.

Her left arm was twisted above her head in an unnatural position. The right arm was completely out of the socket. The head was turned almost completely around. Kevin was oblivious to the weather; his frozen fingers touched the right leg. It was hard, cold, and felt like plastic. He turned to his brother quizzically as John was finishing his conversation on the cell which Kevin didn't even know had rung.

"OK, he'll be glad to hear it. He's freaking out," he heard his brother say as he ended the call. "Kev, it's OK. Barb said she was in the back yard and had just stepped out to look for her cell phone. We took off before she got back is all."

John knelt beside his brother and smiled.

"I didn't think they made these anymore," he said as he lifted his brother to his feet. "Barbie dolls, a little girl's best friend," he chuckled as he picked up the pieces of the doll and put them in his coat pocket.

Kevin was still reeling from the news that his worst fear was not realized. Barb was safe and at home. He thanked God for the second time.

As the two brothers opened the door, the looks on Barb and Linda's faces affirmed they were soaked to the bone and looked like two drowned rats. As they took off their coats, John pulled the pieces of Kacey's toy out of his pocket.

"Mama Baby," Kacey shouted in glee, her chubby little finger pointing to John's hand.

******

City Liquors

I wasted two of the best years of my life in a dark den of iniquity located on the north end of the world-famous Strip in Las Vegas. City Liquors was a bar/casino (seemed like *every* bar in Las Vegas was a casino) that had all the requisite old slot machines and some games you would never see in a *real* casino.

These are just a few of the memories I carry as the seventies came to an end in Sin City.

It was a Saturday night and I had just arrived. The jukebox was blasting away a Conway Twitty tune as the bartender wiped down the old pockmarked wooden bar with his sour towel. Lazily spreading the dirt and alcohol evenly over the surface, he looked up and shouted, "Hey Satin!" He was calling me by my self-appointed nickname the Satin Latin.

Bill had been the 'tender there for about ten years, aging along with the bar that had attracted the oddest assortment of characters ever assembled. At 6 pm, that motley assemblage included Stevie, a good-looking friend of mine who I always felt was "slumming" when he showed up. Like everybody in Las Vegas, Stevie was from "somewhere else." In this case, somewhere else was Minnesota. Stevie worked in a *real* casino with a much better breed of cat both working and gambling there. I would later end up in the same casino plying my trade as a chef.

Theo was another pool-shooting friend of mine I met at City Liquors. He was short, quick, and highly intelligent. I dubbed Theo the Thief and that nickname stuck for all to use. Theo liked the moniker, proudly displaying it on the tattered red sleeve of our 9-ball team shirt. Theo approached me as I made my way to Bill and the V.O. and Budweiser which were calling my name. My raging alcoholism made me a very indiscriminate drinker; I would have drunk a flask of Jabba the Hut's piss if I thought it would get me high.

The strains of Crystal Gayle's *Don't it Make Your Brown Eyes Blue* was drifting above the sounds of jingling coins from the slot trays. The two-foot-deep cloud of smoke which hung perpetually over the two pool tables permeated everything. When I stumbled home, my latest girlfriend was sure I was smoking cigarettes, my rank clothes belying my insistent denials. Anyone who knows me knows how much I hate smoking.

Cigarettes, that is.

"Deadeye!" the shout went out from nearly everyone in the bar. Deadeye was one of the stars of Saturday night at City Liquors. He was about as likeable a guy you would ever want to meet. He would stick his hand out to shake even the dirtiest and sleaziest of people, and he had a way of making you smile through your worst day. He had "the knack" of making you feel better no matter what was on your mind or what the situation.

"Satin!" he shouted out to me. Deadeye liked my nickname Satin Latin and that was the only way he ever addressed me. Deadeye was a hero to me. He was the best 9-ball pool player in a bar full of sharks and league champions. He took me under his wing and taught me how to play 9-ball. He personally turned me into a Top Individual Shooter for our team which represented dingy little City Liquors in the Nevada State 9-ball

Championship Tournament. The run to state was bittersweet, as student bested teacher for the top individual award and I was heartbroken. Deadeye didn't show up to see me lose the title on the last shot of the tournament. As runner-up, I won fifty bucks and a case of Budweiser.

I woke up the next morning in the Las Vegas Metro jail, enduring my second DUI in six weeks.

Zoom to next Saturday night. Zoom past the fact that my girlfriend came to bail me out on Monday but spun around and left when the desk sergeant informed her that I was not alone in the vehicle when I was arrested. The other occupants of the vehicle were: a two-foot Grafix bong and a bowl of Panama Red kickass weed. Twelve empty beer cans littered the back seat. Oh yeah, and a prostitute. I am pretty sure that is why my girlfriend left.

Not the station house.

Me.

"Deadeye!" the shout again went up. The dans macabre continues……

I proceeded to drink the last bottle of V.O. in the bar and switched to drinking tumblers full of Bombay. I lost track of all things normal around midnight. All the gang had dispersed, leaving me and Bill to carry the torch.

Led Zeppelin's *Stairway to Heaven* was blasting now and my head kept time with John

Bonham's drums between gulps of gin. I was now officially blind drunk, struggling to see my own reflection in the cracked mirror behind Bill. I couldn't even *spell* DUI although it was near-certainty number three was soon to occur.

I blinked my eyes several times to get a clearer picture of well, everything, but I remained out-of-focus.

I was contemplating ordering some food from the little toaster grill "kitchen" behind the bar from Chef Bill when I felt a soft touch on my left shoulder.

The lady sat in the torn leather stool beside me and ordered a martini.

She inched closer to me, and I turned to look at her. The lady was not my typical Saturday night prey. She was older than the others and she spoke with a southern accent. Having lived in the south, I figured she was from somewhere around Alabama or Tennessee. She started offering the filthiest sexual proposition I had ever heard, and I began to pay attention. She continued in a most explicit dialogue, and I began to stir in my loins as I drooled on the bar.

Very romantic.

"I'm gonna show you what the young girls don't know," she cooed as my interest grew. "I'm gonna......

The Point of No Return arrived precisely at 3 am and I mumbled something unintelligible to Bill. I placed my hand on the small of the lady's back and swiftly ushered her to my car in the alley.

I am absolutely certain selective memory has filtered this incident through the years, but I still get sick when I recall what happened next.

Flash to my condo in North Las Vegas.

Up the stairs to my bedroom.

My condition did not lend itself to patience or consideration. We threw ourselves on my bed and sweated, writhed, and copulated for the better part of two hours. I do remember attempting to lower her bra for easier access, but she politely refused, pushing my eager rough hands away.

We fell asleep and off we drifted.......

It was nine o'clock in the morning when I stirred awake, my German Shorthaired Pointer Chopper licking me in an effort to get me to fill his dish with yummy dog food. I went downstairs, my companion still under the covers. I fed Chopper and I could hear what's-her-name stirring upstairs.

I lit a joint, popped a Bud, and drained half of it in one desperate gulp.

I ascended the stairs, opened the door to my bedroom, and stopped literally in mid-stride. There, on the bed, getting dressed was.....

"I'm sorry, I stammered. "What is your name?"

"Ruth, she answered.

"Ruth, how old are you?" I had to ask.

"Eighty-nine" she replied.

WTF?

******

X

Since I live in one of the nation's driest areas (Phoenix, Arizona), my first instinct under this difficult heading was xeric, or pertaining to dry or drought-like conditions. However, that might have led to a full-length novel which I am entertaining a notion to write titled "The Last Drop of Water on Earth."

Stay tuned.

Xenophobia is a fear or hatred of others than yourself. I contend there is some self-loathing involved as well. Before one can accept the unknown or unconventional, one must be totally secure in who one is and what the belief structure looks like fodder for yet another of my favorite rants denigrating the ethnocentric, the bigoted, and the biased. This condition affects every human being in every corner of the globe.

I like the pink, cherry Sour Tarts the best, so I too am biased. I still swell with pride at the sight of our flag furling in the desert wind, or while the national anthem plays, which are ethnocentric, by now Pavlovian, reactions for which I offer no apologies. I do love our country with all her faults. Ethnocentrism cloaked under the guise of nationalism.

I wish I could say I have never been bigoted or exhibited such behavior in my life. I have been the giver and receiver of such behavior, and both memories elicit shame, so I prefer not to go there. Ever. I have grown to be a better person than I was, which is all any of us can do. Get better. Be better tomorrow than you were today. As I approach my own denouement, time becomes even more valuable, so be better this afternoon than I was this morning.

For too long in my own life I disassociated myself from the rest of humanity, a long period of personal darkness that embarrassingly, included my own family members.

We'll slip, we'll fall, but at that juncture what are your options?

Quit. Fuck it. Or you pick yourself up and keep fighting the good fight. It is a fight we will never win but as long as you are fighting, *you are winning.*

******

Incredulous

Tony got out of his '68 Corvette and slammed the door as he turned his purple face toward the approaching taxicab driver.

"You idiot," he bellowed. "What the hell is wrong with you? You saw me pulling in and you cut me off! Asshole! Oh great, a dumbass foreigner. I hope you don't expect me to apologize you fuckin' little raghead. Just have your terrorist homeland charge another couple cents at the gas pump! Look what you did to my car." Tony was waving something overhead wildly.

"I apologize; Assan began. I meant no harm sir. I will be more vigilant in the future." The dark brown man extended his skinny arm in a gesture of friendship.

"Get the fuck out of my way," Tony said as he slapped away Assan's hand.

Tony slung the front-left hubcap off his classic Chevy in Assan's direction, and it landed at Assan's feet.

"Hey! Saheeeb! Are you listening to me fool?" Tony was obviously drunk, high, or both. He was teetering and swaying as if he were ready to drop.

It was raining in the city.

Assan stooped to pick up the hubcap, the edges almost razor-sharp due to the peculiarity of the design, with dangerous silver spokes to boot.

"Here you are sir," he said, offering the shiny hubcap as he approached Tony.

"Oh hell no, sandnigger", Tony shot back. "You are buying me a brand new one to replace that bent piece of shit."

"But sir, it was YOU who caused the…." Assan recoiled.

Tony raised his hand to silence the cabbie.

"Wait. I've got something in my trunk just for you." Tony belched as he returned to his 'Vette. He pulled out what looked like a rifle and turned towards Assan. Tony's eyes appeared to be rotating in his big head. He looked like the devil himself, and he was chuckling out loud. He leveled the rifle and slowly lowered his eye to the sight.

"Sir, please," Assan pleaded as Tony closed his left eye.

Assan stepped back and without hesitation, flung the hubcap at Tony like a Frisbee. The sharp edge of the cap sliced cleanly through Tony's neck, severing it.

In a split-second his head fell from his shoulders and hit the greasy pavement with a sickening *thud,* blood gushing from his neck like a geyser.

When the head stopped rolling, you should have seen the look on his face.

******

Y

For the emotion I selected, I use sexual attraction and tension as main components in the very short story *Desire*.

The main character is a doctor, and I want to take this opportunity to "hedge my bets" from some of the previous shots I have taken at the field of medicine.

Do I distrust Big Pharma? Hell yeah! Is there more money in curing or treating maladies? Do I never forget that doctors are healers but also businessmen dependent on long-term visitation and care? Absolutely. If I were dying, would I want my drunk-ass golf buddy or a doctor to assist?

My drunk-ass golf buddy finishes a very close second. Although I do have several friends I golf with that qualify under both headings. And I *know* those fools aren't laying a hand on me.

Not in this lifetime.

I must admit, I looked long and hard at youthful and yielding. I'm for anyone and everyone being, enjoying, and *staying* youthful. All through this crazy ride we call life, youth is NOT the domain of the young. I am not gonna bullshit you, the music thing I do not get. Technology has kicked my ass. However, I still laugh as loud now, smile as wide, and enjoy as much this planet's bounty as I did when I was a twenty-five-year-old. Right. I am having a hard time keeping a straight face. Right?

Yielding is another of my personal traits. Unfortunately, so is unyielding. Both are also foibles. I don't mean yielding in the sense of being nice and yielding the right-of-way to another person, but more in the sense of perhaps not fighting as hard as I was capable of and yielding to other pressures or influences.

Accepting. Untenable. Lazy.

Let's face it, you don't really hear the use of the word yearning in conversation except the dusty old standard "I yearn for the days when…." Something I have not and never will say.

Maybe my Pops' generation.

Days of yore.

Or when you want to select an emotion for your collection of short stories.

******

Desire

Cassie entered the room and stopped dead in her tracks. She crossed the floor and approached the beautiful young woman.

"Hi Colleen," were the only words she could muster as she touched the soft white shoulder of her soon-to-be next girlfriend.

Colleen Chayonne, twenty-three years young and Irish-Canadian, lay on her side motionless. She stirred briefly at Cassie's touch and returned to her slumber.

They had only known each other for a brief ten days, but Cassie had no doubts that the feelings she had for Colleen were real and undeniable. She could only hope that the feelings were mutual and that her irregular breathing was further evidence of that.

"Colleen, is this a good time?" Cassie touched her again, trying to awaken the object of her intense desire. Colleen remained still.

Cassie leaned in closer...closer…closer….

Colleen had auburn hair, as fine as gossamer, royal blue eyes, and a body that would make Venus green with envy. Smooth skin, soft cheeks, pouty blue lips…….Blue lips.

Cyanosis.

"Code Blue!"

Cassie started pounding Colleen's chest in an attempt to resuscitate her patient. She alternately forced air into Colleen's lungs, and performed compressions, finally giving up on CPR and reaching for the defibrillation paddles.

"Paddles!" Cassie shouted. "Clear!"

The alternating current of the defib attempt caused Colleen's body to lift and convulse, then settle back down on the hospital bed.

"Again. Clear!" Cassie looked to the heart monitor and the flatline returned. "Clear!" Cassie shouted in vain sending another high-voltage current through Colleen.

The ICU nurse lightly touched Cassie's shoulder. "She's gone doctor," was all she offered as the monotone was respectfully terminated.

Dr. Cassandra Butler slumped over the lifeless body of Colleen Chayonne.

"Time of death 8:12 am," Cassie proclaimed as she exited the room. *Sometimes I really hate this fucking job* the doctor thought.

******

Z

Zealous will bring my first book to its sunset. The gladiator sport of football is the setting. Football coaches all have different ways of motivating their players through good and bad performances on the gridiron. *Halftime* is an example.

Notre Dame's legendary coach Knute Rockne once left his team sitting alone in the locker room after trailing in the first half. At the very last second before they had to exit the locker room and head to the tunnel, Rockne burst through the door and said in a very high-pitched voice "Let's go girls!"

The team emerged seeing red and ultimately triumphed.

The word zealot, however, has developed into a bit of a dichotomy. To perform with zeal is a highly desired trait but taking on the role of zealot now is colored with such terms as religious, militant, war-like, and fanatic. Now if you are going to include groups like ISIS, Al-Qaeda, and the Taliban, you must surely include the most radical, dangerous, unmovably, singularly focused group of them all (and I'm not talking about Republicans).

I am talking about SEC football fans.

I grew up part of my life in South Carolina, and I really loved it there. Between the fishing, the girls with their sexy drawls, and the bounteous pecan trees, I have often thought fondly of the Palmetto State. I remember when the busing issue was at the forefront of society and our small rural school was directly affected. The student enrollment went from under one-thousand students in grades 9-12 to over five-thousand in the course of a weekend.

There are several stories of this type of situation, the most famous of which would be *Remember the Titans.*

The story of the Hillcrest Wildcats was a bit in the other direction. More *The Longest Yard* than *Titans,* the closest our haplessly undermanned squad came to sniffing a win was against the eventual state runner-up and their high school All-American quarterback. We actually were leading 7-6 at halftime, a result so shocking it was the sports headline the next day in the papers.

We eventually lost 63-7.

******

Halftime

The first half could not have gone worse for the Spartans. They were on the receiving end of an all-out ass-whipping at the hands of the Tigers. The score was 35-0 but it could have been much worse. The players filed into the locker room, and you could hear a pin drop when the coach followed them in and slammed the door behind him.

"You are the worst excuse for a football team I have ever seen! Don't you have any pride? You are playing like a bunch of losers! Are you losers? By the looks of this first half, I would say absolutely yes. You are the most pathetic group of losers I have ever coached. You make me sick. No blocking, no tackling, and no energy. Why don't you just fucking quit?"

"Bill, what a stupid play you made giving up that touchdown when you could have just wrapped their halfback up in the backfield. You're slow, stupid, and a waste of skin! Pat, you call yourself a quarterback? My dog *shits* better quarterbacks than you! Henry, I hope you jack off better than you block, or you are in for a shitty life. Richard, I wouldn't cross the street to piss on you if you were on fire. You're not worth my, or any of the other coaches' time. Quit fucking around and run the football like we taught you. Gentlemen get your heads out of your asses, or I'll kick your heads up so far, you'll never be able to pull them out. Your play in the first half makes me want to puke."

The coach looked at his starting linebacker Matt Johnson who also had a rough first half. Matt raised his hand.

"Don't you fucking *move* Matt. You are a pussy. My own daughter can hit harder than you. You are a piece of shit. Now I'm not asking you, I'm telling you:

You *are* going to play hard in the second half and don't even think about quitting! I will run you into the ground at practice on Monday and if you don't show up, consider your resignation from this football team. Now get your fucking lazy asses back out there."

As the players sulked their way back to the slaughter, linebackers coach Ed Steen approached the head coach.

"Coach, pretty rough halftime speech. Think it might've been a little too much?"

"Not rough enough in my opinion, Coach. Why?"

"Well, because this is Pop Warner and they're only eight years old."

******

The End